Julius Althaus

On Paralysis, Neuralgia, and other Affections of the Nervous System

SALZWASSER
VERLAG

Julius Althaus

On Paralysis, Neuralgia, and other Affections of the Nervous System

Reprint of the original, first published in 1864.

1st Edition 2022 | ISBN: 978-3-75259-449-2

Verlag (Publisher): Salzwasser Verlag GmbH, Zeilweg 44, 60439 Frankfurt, Deutschland
Vertretungsberechtigt (Authorized to represent): E. Roepke, Zeilweg 44, 60439 Frankfurt, Deutschland
Druck (Print): Books on Demand GmbH, In de Tarpen 42, 22848 Norderstedt, Deutschland

ON

PARALYSIS, NEURALGIA,

AND OTHER AFFECTIONS OF THE NERVOUS SYSTEM;

AND THEIR SUCCESSFUL TREATMENT BY

GALVANISATION AND FARADISATION.

BY

JULIUS ALTHAUS, M.D.

Third Edition.

LONDON

1864.

PREFACE.

A Third Edition of this Book having been called for, I have carefully revised it, and made numerous additions, both scientific and practical; and I now submit it again to the Profession, in the hope that the facts and opinions I have advanced may serve to extend the knowledge of this important branch of Medicine.

18, Bryanston Street,
Portman Square,
January, 1864.

TABLE OF CONTENTS.

CHAPTER I.

CHAPTER II.

CHAPTER III.

CHAPTER IV.

ON PARALYSIS,

ETC.

CHAPTER I.

1. The history of the therapeutical use of electricity, galvanism, electro-magnetism, and magneto-electricity, is identical with that of the discoveries made of the physical, chemical, and physiological properties of these different agents. Electricity has, in fact, been medically employed as long as it has been known. The torpedo, or electric ray, which, when touched at any part, and more especially at the fins, gives a shock analogous to that yielded by the Leyden jar, was used in antiquity for the cure of headaches and gout, and highly recommended by Scribonius Largus, a Physician of the time of the Emperor Tiberius. Pliny mentions the electricity of this fish as a valuable therapeutical agent, and Dioscorides has recorded a case of prolapsus ani which was cured by it. In the same manner the

negresses, in certain parts of Africa, have from time immemorial been accustomed to place weak and sickly children in pools of water containing electric fishes.

ELECTRISATION.

2. After the invention of the ordinary electrical machine, in which electricity is produced by the friction of a glass plate or cylinder between cushions; and still more after that of the Leyden jar, Medical men in Germany, France, and England turned their attention to the therapeutical use of an agent evidently so powerful. A German Physician of the last century was the first to describe a case of paralysis cured by sparks drawn from the electrical machine (1744). Jallabert, the Abbé Sans, Mauduit, Sigaud de la Fond, and Cavallo, afterwards used and preconised the same means for almost every form of disease: and a few Italian practitioners, not satisfied with the effects of electricity alone, resorted to the ludicrous device of using in their machines glass cylinders filled with Peruvian balsam, purgatives and various other medicines, which were believed to be endowed with tenfold power if introduced into the system in so subtle a manner.

3. The method of applying frictional electricity, which is even at the present day sometimes used, is as follows:—The patient is placed upon an insulating stool, and made to take hold of the prime conductor of the electrical machine. Sparks are then drawn from the body either by the hand of the operator or by metallic conductors. By this proceeding a sharp pricking or pungent sensation is produced at the points touched; and after a time the skin is reddened and an eruption, resembling lichen urticatus, breaks out. In the electricity room of Guy's Hospital, where formerly, under the superintendence of Dr. Golding Bird and Dr. Gull, electricity was extensively employed, the usual practice was to take sparks from the spine in the following way: a brass ball, furnished with a wire or chain in connection with the ground, was passed up and down in the direction of the spine of the patient, who was seated on an insulating stool, while the machine was in action. By this means sparks were made to pass from the skin to the brass ball, and thence escaped through the wire or chain to the ground. Shocks from the Leyden jar were especially employed in the treatment of amenorrhœa, when they were directed through the pelvis. No doubt

the electrical machine and the Leyden jar have afforded relief in certain affections of the nervous system, in which it may be presumed that the use of any counter-irritant would prove beneficial; but they are powerless in a number of other affections, in which galvanism and electro-magnetism find their appropriate sphere of action.

GALVANISATION.

4. Amongst the numerous discoveries made in the last decennia of the eighteenth century, one which has proved of surpassing importance for scientific and practical purposes, was that of galvanism (1786). The fundamental fact is, that a continuous electric current is produced by the chemical action of two heterogeneous conducting bodies. After this had once been established, the discovery of the voltaic pile (1800), of electro-magnetism and magneto-electricity (1831), were the natural consequence. The nature of these several agents, and their relations to the animal economy, have, by a series of laborious experiments, protracted over the space of more than half a century, been in a great measure unveiled, and thus not only an infinite number of most important physical and physiological discoveries

have been rendered possible which could not have been made by any other means, but also remedial agents obtained which, although not more wonderful in their effects than quinine, iodine and digitalis, are of the greatest intrinsic value, and which, in the treatment of many affections, cannot be replaced by any other.

5. Shortly after galvanism had been discovered, therapeutical experiments were undertaken with it, and a copious literature on its medical virtues soon sprang up, amongst which the treatises of Grapengiesser, Jacobs, Augustin and Aldini, deserve special mention. The physical, chemical, and physiological properties of galvanism, as they became successively known in course of time, excited the imagination of Physicians and laymen in an equally powerful manner; and it was concluded that so marvellous an agent must needs possess wonderful curative powers. It is difficult, at the present time, to imagine the enthusiasm, bordering on intoxication, for the newly-discovered remedial agent, which reigned in the commencement of the present century, and the unbounded expectations which were entertained as to its therapeutical value. It was not only recommended and used for almost all diseases which

exist, but was also believed to be able to rescue from death persons who had just been hanged or drowned.

6. Of the physiological action of the galvanic current upon the different tissues of the human body very little was known. The voltaic pile was indiscriminately applied, even for such diseases in which it must have done harm; moreover, the power of this apparatus is, for reasons which I have explained in my "Treatise on Medical Electricity," very variable, and after a certain time entirely disappears, so that there was sometimes no current at all, while at others there was either a weak or a very strong current, and, by the use of the latter, accidents of a serious character were produced. The confidence in the curative powers of galvanism was, therefore, soon entirely shaken, and the voltaic pile ranged together with talismans, amulets, animal magnetism, and mesmerism, amongst the curative treasures of the quacks.

7. Further physical and physiological discoveries on the nature and properties of galvanism were evidently necessary before it could be employed with a fair chance of success in the treatment of disease. It was in Italy that some time afterwards the physiological part of the subject

was more thoroughly investigated, especially by Nobili, Marianini, and Matteucci; while Becquerel in France, Daniell and Grove in England, and Bunsen in Germany, invented galvanic batteries which furnished a much more constant current, and one, therefore, more applicable for Medical purposes than that yielded by the original voltaic pile. Sarlandière made a great step towards improving the mode of applying the galvanic current by using acupuncture needles, whereby the current is allowed to penetrate more deeply into the tissues, and at the same time is limited to those parts requiring the galvanic stimulus. By means of this proceeding, Magendie effected some remarkable cures of paralysis, amaurosis, and neuralgia. It having become known that galvanism may cause the blood to coagulate, Guérard and Pravaz proposed curing aneurisms by galvanopuncture. Wires rendered incandescent by the galvanic current were employed for cauterisation by Heider, Middeldorpff, and Amussat. Others succeeded by the same means in decomposing urinary calculi, and in promoting the growth of healthy granulations and the cicatrisation of ulcers.

FARADISATION.

8. In 1831, Faraday discovered that electric currents of instantaneous duration are induced in conducting-wires by the passage of an ordinary galvanic current (electro-magnetism), as well as by the approach to, and withdrawal from, conducting-wires, of a permanent magnet of steel (magneto-electricity). By this discovery new agents of remarkable power were added to the electric stock, and which were, in course of time, proved to possess physical, chemical, and physiological properties entirely different from those of the continuous galvanic current. Our knowledge of the physical phenomena connected with electro-magnetism and magneto-electricity was considerably enlarged by the researches of Professor Dove, Henry, Becquerel, and De la Rive; and Weber, Valentin, Dubois-Reymond, Helmholtz. Ludwig, Claude Bernard, and many others, zealously investigated the physiological effects of these newly-discovered currents. Machines especially designed for their therapeutical application were constructed by Messrs. Pixii, Saxton, Clarke, Keil, Legendre and Morin, Siemens and Halske, Stöhrer, and many others; while to Duchenne belongs the merit of

having first effectually directed the attention of the medical profession to the therapeutical use of induction currents, the methodical application of which was called by him "Faradisation," in honour of Faraday, the discoverer of this form of electricity.

9. I have already mentioned that the physical, chemical, and physiological effects of the continuous galvanic, and of the interrupted (Faradic) current, are entirely different; from which it may be inferred that we cannot expect beneficial results from an indiscriminate use of either of these agents, each one of which has its own special sphere of action. To give only one instance, the continuous galvanic current, if applied to any part of the face, excites the retina in a remarkable manner, so that the person subjected to the operation perceives a flash of light, the intensity of which is directly proportional to the power of the current employed, and inversely proportional to the resistance offered to the passage of the current. A flash is produced by the application to the face of a very feeble continuous current, such as is excited by the contact of a half-crown piece and a penny; it is much more distinct if, instead of this arrangement, zinc and silver, or

zinc and gold, are used; and if the current, furnished by a number of large plates, as in Grove's or Daniell's battery, were used, instantaneous blindness might be the result. If the skin of the face is dry, the flash is less vivid than if it be previously moistened, which diminishes the resistance to the passage of the current. Moreover, the flash is stronger if the conductors are directed to the conjunctiva, or to the Schneiderian membrane, or to the mucous membrane of the cavity of the mouth, than if they are applied to the skin of the face; since the delicate epithelium of the mucous membranes offers much less resistance to the passage of the current than the epidermis. This same continuous galvanic current has only little action upon the muscles of the face, while, on the other hand, the interrupted Faradic current has little or no action upon the retina, and a powerful effect upon the muscles. These facts are of great practical importance, as it follows from them that we may use the interrupted current without danger in paralysis of the portio dura, for exciting the paralysed muscles of the face, and that we must avoid in this affection the application of the continuous galvanic current, as thereby the vision of the patient might be endangered, while no good would be done to the facial paralysis. Other facts relating to the difference in the effects of galvanism and electro-magnetism will be mentioned hereafter.

GALVANIC AND FARADIC MACHINES.

10. A most important point for the practitioner who intends using electricity as a remedy, is the choice of good apparatus furnishing a continuous, electro-magnetic and magneto-electric current; and, the want of success of an electric treatment has, in many instances, been due to the insufficiency of the machines employed. I shall first consider the apparatus by which a continuous current is furnished, and then pass on to the Faradic or induction machines.

(*a.*) *Continuous Galvanic Current.*—I consider the following requisites indispensable for machines of this kind. (1.) They should furnish a large quantity of electricity. (2.) The current should not be subjected to any considerable variations within a certain time (say twelve hours). (3.) The apparatus should be handy and fit for use in the consulting and sick room. 4. The dose of electricity to be given should be able to be exactly, nicely, and easily measured. In the machines which were formerly in use, most or all of these qualities were wanting, and they were, therefore, unfit for medical use. The original voltaic pile has been entirely given up, as it is not only very troublesome and inconvenient, but the current yielded by it is subject to considerable variations. Cruikshanck's battery is more easily manipulated, but its current is likewise inconstant. The galvanic poultice of M. Récamier, and the electric belt of Messrs. Breton, are ingenious inventions, but they suffer from the same defects as the voltaic pile. Pulvermacher's chains, which are still much used, have the great drawback of furnishing only a comparatively small quantity of electricity, while they have a high tension; moreover, the current yielded by them is extremely inconstant and unreliable. The only batteries by which a really constant current is furnished, and which should therefore be exclusively used by medical men, are those of Daniell, Grove, and Bunsen. Until very recently, however, these batteries were only constructed for physical and chemical laboratories, or for the purpose of galvanic cauterisation. The only machine which as yet seems to me to combine all the necessary requisites mentioned above, is one which has recently been constructed, according to my directions, by Messrs. Legendre and Morin, of Paris, and which is Bunsen's battery modified with special regard to medical practice. In this machine, which I exhibited at a recent meeting of the Medical Society of London, there is a very considerable quantity of electricity, which, as is well known, depends upon the extent of surface exposed to the chemical action of the liquids contained in the battery. Each cell is four inches high, and has a circumference of five inches. The carbon used in it is that known as Deleuil's carbon, which affords every advantage that can be reasonably desired. This peculiar kind of carbon is prepared from the deposit formed in the Paris gas-works, and is distinguished by its hardness, uniformity, durability, and its property of giving, with nitric acid and zinc, a very constant galvanic current; one such cell, if charged with 50 per cent. nitric acid, is sufficient to put into action powerful induction machines. There are thirty cells in this machine, which is therefore one of great force; for, in most cases, from five to twenty cells are quite sufficient. Moreover, the apparatus, though somewhat heavy from the great quantity of zinc contained in it, is portable and perfectly clean. There is no escape of acid fumes, as the cells are entirely closed up by a cover of hardened gutta-percha. Finally, the dose of electricity to be given may be exactly measured. The plates which establish the connection between the several cells are perforated, so that conducting wires may be stuck into any of them, and thus, at a moment's notice, a current of any power may be administered. The machine is, in fact, perfect in its kind, the only drawback to it being the loss of time which is unavoidably attached to charging and discharging the cells, but which, with some little practice, may be reduced to a minimum.

(*b.*) *Electro-Magnetism and Magneto-Electricity.* —The induction machines used for medical purposes are either volta-electric or magneto-electric (rotatory). The former have the advantage of being self-acting, and of allowing an extremely nice regulation, not only of the intensity of the current, but also of the rapidity of the intermittences. Rotatory machines were believed to be superior to those just mentioned, on account of their being cleaner and always ready for action, but these two properties are by no means wanting in the volta-electric machines of recent construction, amongst which that made by Messrs. Stöhrer, of Dresden, may be mentioned as a specimen of what induction machines ought to be. It would, however, be erroneous to suppose that the current induced by voltaic electricity, and that induced by a permanent magnet of steel possess exactly the same physiological and therapeutical properties. Such is not the case, and the reason will be readily understood, if we consider that the variations in the density of the volta-electric current are far more sudden than those of the magneto-electric current. The former, therefore, acts more on the motor nerves and muscles, while the magneto-electric current acts more on the optic nerve, and is more beneficial in the cure of rheumatic callosities. The chief properties which induction machines suited for the treatment of disease should possess are, that the dose of electricity may be exactly measured to suit the different constitutions, age and sex of the patients, and the more or less severe degree of the affection for which it is employed; that both the current of the thick and of the fine wire should be obtainable; and that the rheotome or cut-current should be so constructed as to allow of slow and rapid interruptions, *ad libitum*, and should not easily get out of order.

CHAPTER II.

11. The continuous galvanic current, which always moves in the same direction, possesses considerable chemical effects, as it easily decomposes water and saline solutions, oxygen and acids being attracted to the positive pole, while hydrogen and alkalies accumulate at the negative pole. On the contrary, induction currents, which move alternately in different directions, have only a slight chemical action, for as each wire serves alternately as positive and negative pole, their chemical effects are, in a great measure, neutralized as soon as produced. Thus, if induction currents are made to act upon water, both hydrogen and oxygen appear simultaneously at either of the polcs; and, being in the nascent state, immediately combine again to form water. *If we, therefore, wish to make use of the chemical effects of electricity, it follows that the continuous galvanic current alone should be used.* This applies chiefly to the electric treatment of aneurisms and varices, which has not yet been so extensively

resorted to as the advantages connected with it seem to warrant.

ANEURISMS AND VARICES.

12. By making a continuous current act upon blood, we may cause it to coagulate, not only when taken out of an artery, vein, or capillary vessels, but also while still circulating in the living body. Clots may thus be produced at a given point in the circulating system, those of venous blood being less firm and more dark than those of arterial blood. *Clots, are, however, only produced at the positive pole*, where, in consequence of the decomposition of the salines contained in the blood, acids are liberated. Alkali accumulates at the negative pole, where, therefore, the blood is rendered more fluid. Thus it is obvious that surgeons cannot be successful in the electric treatment of aneurism, if, as has repeatedly been done, induction currents, which have only trifling chemical effects, are employed instead of the continuous current, and if, instead of the positive pole, both poles, or the negative pole, is made to act upon the blood. Moreover, M. Steinlein has drawn attention to the circumstance that the nature of the metal of which the needles used in

such proceedings are made, has a certain influence upon the effects produced. If the needle connected with the positive pole is of platinum, coagulation proceeds slowly; if the platinum needle has a point of iron, the effect is quicker; and the action is most rapid if a needle of zinc, or a steel needle covered with a layer of zinc be used. This is due to the fact, that the acid liberated at the positive pole forms chemical compounds with the metals of which the needles are made, and the coagulation of fibrine is favoured, if chloride of zinc is acting on the blood.

As clots which are rapidly formed, are always softer than those which are slowly produced, it is important that the operation should not last longer than about five minutes, if aneurisms are to be treated by this proceeding. If the current is allowed to pass through the aneurismal sac for twenty minutes or longer, the sac is quite closed up, and the clot thus formed is liable to be again dissolved, as it consists of fibrine and blood-globules; while if the clot is slowly produced, it is exclusively formed of fibrine, and is therefore hard, and tends to rapid organization.

M. Pétrequin, of Lyons, was the first to cure aneurisms by this proceeding (1845); and since then other successful cases have been published. The galvanic treatment of aneurisms is especially to be recommended in such cases where other methods cannot be conveniently applied on account of the seat of the tumour. In *varices*, where the ordinary modes of treatment are so frequently unsuccessful, Galvanisation would be more even generally useful than in aneurisms.

HYDROCELE.

13. In cases where the absorption of effusions in superficial tissues is to be promoted, both Galvanisation and Faradisation may be advantageously employed. Thus, cases of hydrocele, in which both the injection of iodine and the seton had failed, have been cured by the use of either of these methods. Faradisation is, however, preferable from being less troublesome. The proceeding in hydrocele should be as follows:—two acupuncture needles are introduced, the one into the upper, and the other into the lower part of the tumour; and the free extremities of the needles are then connected with the poles of the induction machine. The current should only begin to act after the introduction of the needles, because, otherwise, violent pain would be caused on lodging them in the sac.

We must also take care that the points of the needles should project into the fluid, as, if they are merely passed into the subcutaneous cellular tissue, or the tunica dartos, the current would only act upon these membranes, but not upon the tunica vaginalis and the fluid accumulated in its sac. At first, a mild current should be used, which may be gradually increased, until the patient complains of pain. The operation should last for about twenty minutes; at the same time gentle pressure may be exercised upon the tumour. Immediately after the operation, the scrotum appears puffed, and the quantity of fluid in the sac is diminished. Sometimes the hydrocele disappears within the twenty-four hours after the first operation; in other cases, three or four operations are required for effecting a cure.

OPACITIES OF THE CORNEA.

14. In opacities of the cornea, especially such as defy other therapeutical proceedings, Faradisation is a valuable remedy. Galvanisation may also be useful; but it must be applied with special caution, because of the peculiar action of the continuous current upon the retina. It is, therefore necessary, if the latter be used, that the current should be of

very low tension, such as is furnished by from four to six cells of Bunsen's battery. The induced current only acts upon the retina, if it possesses a very high tension, and even then, not nearly so much as the continuous current. In order to discover the relative value of the different modes of treating opacities of the cornea, Dr. A. Von Graefe used, in patients in whom both eyes were similarly effected, the induced current on the one, and laudanum, nitrate of silver, etc., on the other, with the result that the cure by Faradisation was much more rapid than by the other means.

15. Opacities of the cornea invariably require a somewhat protracted treatment, viz., from one to three months, according to the severity of the affection. The cure is more rapid if the operations succeed each other at short intervals, as every other day, or four times a week, from ten minutes to a quarter of an hour each time. The following case may serve to illustrate the therapeutical proceeding:—

Case 1.—Mr. H. T., aged 19, received in May, 1862, a violent blow on the left temple, from a cricket ball. He was at first completely stunned, and he felt great pain in the head for several days afterwards. The conjunctiva and cornea of the left eye soon became much inflamed, for which the patient was put under a course of mercury; but although his system was much affected by the medicine, the eye did not get better. Mercury was therefore given up after a time, and other treatment resorted to. The inflammation then gradually subsided, but there remained a considerable opacity, which covered the whole extent of the cornea, and was thickest in the lower part of that membrane, whereby vision was almost entirely prevented. Mr. White Cooper, whom the patient consulted in July, 1862, believed that Faradisation would be the best means of promoting the absorption of this opacity, and sent the patient to me. I employed Faradisation combined with a continuous current of low tension, the negative pole being directed to the closed eye, and the positive to the temple, thus stimulating the influence of the first branch of the trigeminal nerve upon the nutritive processes in the eye. The patient quickly improved under this treatment; and when he discontinued it, after having had twenty-four operations, there merely remained a very thin film on the cornea, which was only perceptible on close examination, and impeded vision but little. A complete cure would probably have been effected, if the patient, who did not live in town, had been able to pursue the treatment for some time longer.

CATARACT.

16. If the zinc pole of a voltaic pile is made to act upon the lens of the eye, this is rendered opaque; and if the copper pole is afterwards directed to it, the opacity again disappears. This fact induced M. Crussel to recommend Galvanisation for the cure of cataract; but since, in the few cases which have thus been treated, inflammation of the choroidea, iris, and retina, and destruction of the eye-ball have followed the operation, it would be unjustifiable to resort to it.

TUMOURS.

17. Faradisation and Galvanisation may be usefully employed for certain tumours, especially of the glandular kind, and some forms of struma; and are chiefly to be recommended where surgical operations are impracticable, on account of the seat of the tumour, or where the patient is averse to such operations. A striking case of this kind occurred a short time ago in the practice of Professor Langenbeck, and Dr. Meyer, of Berlin. The patient suffered from a hard glandular tumour, as

large as the head of an adult, and lodged between the head and the right shoulder, filling up the space between the lower jaw, the mastoid process, and the linea semicircularis inferior of the occipital bone, and extending backwards in the direction of the vertebral column, which was dislodged towards the left side. The circumference of the left side of the neck was only six inches, while that of the right side was no less than fourteen. After fifty-six applications of the induced current, the tumour was reduced to one-half of its previous size, and by further treatment its bulk was still more diminished. In such cases, each operation should last for about an hour, and the treatment must be persevered in for a considerable time if beneficial results are to be obtained. Galvanisation seems, in the treatment of these affections, equally valuable as Faradisation.

STRICTURES OF THE URETHRA.

18. Messrs. Willebrandt, Wertheimer, and Jacksch have recommended and used galvanism for the cure of *strictures of the urethra.* An insulated catheter, with a free metallic point, is introduced into the urethra, so that it touches the stricture; and it is then connected with the nega-

tive pole of the battery. For establishing the circuit, a conductor connected with the positive pole is placed in the hand of the patient. The catheter is left in the urethra for from ten to twenty minutes, after which it easily glides into the bladder. From eight to ten such operations are said to be sufficient for the cure of severe strictures; but further experience is required before a decided opinion on the value of Galvanisation in cases of this kind can be given.

ULCERS, DECUBITUS, ETC.

19. For ulcers, in which the secretion is of an unsatisfactory character; and in which a growth of healthy granulations is to be promoted, both Galvanisation and Faradisation may be advantageously employed. A single pair of zinc and silver, as recommended by Mr. Spencer Wells, may be used, the silver being applied to the ulcer, and the zinc to any part of the skin, which must be previously moistened in order to facilitate the passage of the current. By this means a very beneficial change in the condition of ulcers is often effected within twenty-four hours. The surface beneath the silver rapidly cicatrises, while that beneath the zinc is converted into a super-

ficial eschar. By frequently changing the position of the zinc pole, the unpleasant effects of the latter may be almost entirely counterbalanced.

20. Faradisation is likewise exceedingly useful where ulcers are slow to heal; and after amputations, where the stump is in a bad condition. Some years ago, I treated by this means a patient upon whom Mr. Wells had performed amputation of the forefinger. Cicatrisation had been very tardy, and although the wound healed at last, the stump remained livid, very soft, was exceedingly sensitive to touch, and bled easily. Under the influence of Faradisation, it became much firmer, acquired a healthier colour, was less sensitive to touch, and never bled again. Mr. Mitchell Henry has informed me that he has, in patients who were under his care in the Middlesex Hospital, found the same means very beneficial for improving the secretion of ulcers; and Dr. Ruschenberger, of the United States' Navy, has successfully used the electric current for the cure of unmanageable decubitus. Mr. Nunn, of the Middlesex Hospital, has also adopted this mode of treatment for the sequelae of mammary abscess, in sinus of the breast, and the painful

œdema, which is so apt to remain after the more acute phenomena of inflammation have subsided. In several instances, Mr. Nunn has seen, after one application, the indolent edges of the fistulous opening assuming a healthy appearance, and the dull red colour of the infiltrated skin giving place to a tint peculiar to resolution. In all these cases, Faradisation acts by stimulating the vasomotor nerves, in consequence of which the activity of the blood-vessels is increased, and the absorption of exudation-products is promoted.

URINARY CALCULI.

21. Calculi of the most different chemical composition may be dissolved or disintegrated by means of electricity. Mr. Robinson has recommended the mechanical action of an electric discharge from the Leyden jar, for destroying the texture of the calculus. Such a proceeding, however ingenious, would yet not seem devoid of danger, since small fragments of the stone might by the force of the shock be lodged in the tissue of the bladder Prévost and Dumas have employed the mechanical action of torrents of hydrogen and oxygen, developed by the decomposition of water by means of the continuous current, for

rendering calculi friable. Again, M. Bonnet and Dr. Bence Jones have proved that we may, by the electro-chemical decomposition of a solution of nitrate of potash, convey acids and alkalies to the stone, without diffusing these powerful solvents in the urine contained in the bladder, which latter would therefore not be injured by such an operation. We know that most urinary calculi may be dissolved either by nitric acid or by potash. If, therefore, a calculus is immersed in a solution of nitrate of potash, and a continuous galvanic current is caused to act upon this solution, nitric acid will be attracted to the positive pole, and caustic potash to the negative pole. Thus, one side of the calculus will be subjected to the action of the acid, and the other to that of the alkali; so that, if the stone be composed of phosphates, it will be dissolved on the acid side; and if composed of uric acid or urate of ammonia, it will be dissolved on the alkaline side. No doubt, this proceeding might be highly advantageous, especially for the removal of large calculi, for which lithotrity is not applicable; but it has hitherto been found impossible to construct an instrument by means of which the current could be safely conveyed to the calculus, and which at the same time prevented the liquid in the bladder from assuming a high temperature, and allowed of the escape of the gases which are formed by the decomposition of water. Dr. Melicher, of Vienna, affirms having successfully operated by Galvanisation upon two patients suffering from stone; but as he has not given a full description of his cases, nor of the instruments employed by him, his statement is devoid of value.

THE ELECTRO-CHEMICAL BATH.

22. The electro-chemical bath has been recommended for extracting from the human body, by the aid of a voltaic pile of about thirty pairs, various metallic substances which have been taken as remedies, or lodged in the system, while being used in the different arts and trades in which they are required. It is administered in the following way:—the patient is placed up to his neck in a large metallic tub, which is filled with water and insulated from the ground, and one end of which is, by means of a screw, connected with the negative pole of a pile of thirty pairs of plates; the patient sits in this tub upon a bench of wood, insulated from the tub, and having the length of the body, and he holds the positive pole of the

battery alternately in the right and in the left hand. The positive electrode is made of iron and covered with linen, in order to diminish the calorific action of the pile, which is very powerful, and whereby the hand might be burnt. The galvanic current now enters the body by the right or left arm; and, according to M. Poey's graphic description, it circulates from the head to the feet, traverses all the internal organs (*sic*), and even the bones, seizes every particle of metal which may exist anywhere, restores it to its primitive form, and deposits it on the whole surface of the sides of the tub, from the neck to the feet.

23. There are, however, very strong reasons for doubting the supposed efficiency of the "electro-chemical bath." In the first place, it is difficult to understand how the galvanic current could convey into the liquid of the bath, and diffuse on the whole surface of the sides of the tub, metallic atoms which, according to the established laws of electro-chemistry, ought to be deposited only on the surface of the electrodes. In the second instance, it is quite evident, that M. Poey is entirely mistaken in supposing that the galvanic current traverses the bones of the patient sitting in the bath. For supporting this view, he quotes Duchenne, who says, that if moistened

conductors connected with the poles of an electrical apparatus are placed upon the surface of a bone, a strong pain of a peculiar character is produced. Hence M. Poey concludes, that if the skin merely be sufficiently moistened, the electric current will traverse the bones. It is scarcely necessary to point out, that the pain produced by placing moistened electrodes on the surface of a bone, is caused by the electric excitation of the nerves of the periosteum; and that, as the bones conduct sixteen to twenty-two times worse than the muscles and other moist tissues of the human body, the current will never traverse the bones of a patient sitting in an electric bath, but will run along the best conducting substances, viz., muscular and cellular tissue. More satisfactory proofs than have up the present time been given, are therefore required, before we can receive the statements as to cures of diseases by means of this proceeding.

INTRODUCTION OF MEDICINAL SUBSTANCES INTO THE SYSTEM BY THE AID OF GALVANISM.

24. Fabré-Palaprat was the first to conceive that it might be possible to introduce medicinal substances into the human body by the aid of elec-

tricity. From some experiments he performed, he concluded that iodine could be conveyed through the human body, from the negative pole of a volcanic pile to the positive pole; but no doubt he has been mistaken in this, as no trustworthy observer after him has been able to verify his results. Further experiments on this point have been made by Drs. Klenke, Hassenstein, and Richardson; but the result has been that electricity neither retards nor accelerates the absorption of medicines, and its use, with regard to this, has therefore been entirely given up.

THE GALVANIC CAUTERY.

25. Wires rendered incandescent by the continuous galvanic current can be employed for producing the effects of the actual cautery, whether we intend destroying the tissues or merely modifying their vitality. In certain cases, the galvanic cautery has great advantages over other cauteries and the knife. It acts rapidly and energetically—it causes little or no hæmorrhage—there is no danger of its hurting the adjacent structures, neither on first introducing nor in afterwards removing it—it favours the growth of healthy granulations, and is not so terrible to the patient as the red-hot iron;

and deeply-seated tissues which are inaccessible to the knife may, by the galvanic cautery, be burnt or cut without danger. After its use the condition of the patient is almost always satisfactory, besides which the proceeding is scarcely painful. The drawback to the galvanic cautery is, that a special and somewhat expensive apparatus is required for its use, and that the wires, when rendered incandescent, may melt, especially if they come in contact with bones or cartilages. The galvanic cautery is chiefly applicable in the following conditions:—Hæmorrhage from a large surface (as from fungus medullaris), certain forms of neuralgia, ulcer of the collum uteri, cancer, fistula, severe stricture of the urethra, and polypus of the uterus, the larynx, and posterior nares. Professor Middeldorpff's galvanic burner, porte-ligature, and seton, are the most convenient instruments for cauterisation by means of galvanism.

INFLUENCE OF ELECTRICITY ON SECRETION.

26. Faradisation, as well as Galvanisation, have a considerable influence upon the process of secretion in different organs. Suppressed perspiration of the feet may by this means be re-established;

and in deficient secretion of semen, Faradisation of the testicles proves useful.

27. In *amenorrhœa* the induced current is a valuable emmenagogue, especially in young unmarried women, in whom we are led to assume a torpid state of the vasomotor nerves of the ovaries and the uterus; and also in cases where the catamenia have been suppressed in consequence of emotion, anxiety, cold, etc. In certain cases of chronic metritis connected with amenorrhœa, absorption of the effusion in the tissue of the uterus takes place under the influence of the same treatment, and the catamenial function then returns to its normal state. In amenorrhœa Faradisation of the womb itself is most effective; but where this is not expedient, the stimulus may be directed to the skin of the soles of the feet and the legs, and by moistened conductors, to the nape of the neck and the os pubis, as well as to the inner surface of the thighs.

28. In women, after parturition, where the *secretion of milk* is tardy, or when it has been suppressed in consequence of emotion, etc., Faradisation of the mammæ by moistened conductors produces beneficial effects; in such cases the operation should last for a quarter of an hour or

twenty minutes; and, if necessary, be several times repeated. From some cases of this kind which have fallen under my observation, and in which the result has been highly satisfactory, I select the following one:—

Case 2. A. B., a lady in good circumstances, aged 31, had her first child in June, 1860. Parturition had been somewhat protracted, but no operation had been necessary. Both mammae were extremely painful, hard, and hot; there had been no trace of colostrum, neither before nor after parturition. The patient had, in the evening and the morning, sensations as if the milk were rising, but in spite of the usual local and internal treatment, there was no flow. Six days after delivery, I applied Faradisation by means of moistened conductors to both mammæ for about twenty minutes. The following morning the milk appeared, although not yet abundantly. The child being now made to suck the breast at short intervals, the secretion soon became quite sufficient, and remained in a satisfactory condition. In this case a single operation had produced the desired result; but generally three or four such applications are necessary.

RHEUMATISM.

29. In acute and chronic rheumatism of the muscles, both Faradisation and Galvanisation, if properly employed, are invaluable remedies. I have frequently cured cases of very long standing, and in which the patients themselves had almost despaired of a cure, by one or two operations. The curative influence of Faradisation is most striking in rheumatism of the deltoid muscle, and of the interossei and lumbricals of the hand, whether of recent origin or of long standing; and in the treatment of these affections, it cannot be replaced by any other remedy.

30. Rheumatic effusions in the joints are likewise amenable to Faradisation, which must in this instance be continued somewhat longer than is necessary for the relief of muscular rheumatism. If, however, the effusions are considerable, Galvanisation is preferable to Faradisation; and both remedies must be used together, if muscular contractions are at the same time present. These contractions, which so frequently resist the ordinary local and internal treatment, are readily cured by a proper use of the continuous and induced (faradic) current.

Case 3. T. C., a musician, aged 31, had, during a tour in Scotland, in the summer of 1859, contracted violent rheumatism, chiefly in the right shoulder and arm, which prevented him from following his occupation. He had been subjected to various coursesof treatment, and had taken large quantities of nitre, bicarbonate of soda, iodide of potassium, and guajac. The pain was relieved after a time, but it never entirely left him, and a considerable contraction of the flexor muscles both of the arm and forearm remained, against which all remedies proved of no avail. He consulted me in September, 1861, when I found the arm in the following condition:—sensation was very dull all over the arm, as the patient did not feel the prick of a pin, nor could he distinguish the two points of the aesthesiometer when held at the usual distance. There was a dull aching pain, which at times became acute, and was very severe as soon as the patient was in bed. Great numbness in the fingers was complained of. The biceps and brachialis internus muscles were so contracted, that the arm was flexed in an angle of about 65°, and could not be extended; the flexor digitorum communis was also rigid, although in a less considerable degree, and the interossei and lumbricals were so much wasted, that the hand was almost entirely useless. The bulk of both arm and forearm was considerably diminished; it was only 10½ inches at a point 8 inches downwards from the acromion, and only 9 inches at a point 3 inches downwards from the olecranon; the corresponding numbers for the left arm being 13 and 10¼. The general health of the patient was pretty good, but there was still want of appetite, and the urine was loaded with urates. I prescribed Vichy water to be taken internally, and the combined use of Faradisation and Galvanisation of the right arm. The result of this treatment was most satisfactory. In the course of a week, under the influence of Faradisation, the pain disappeared. Soon afterwards, the rigidity of the muscles began to subside, sensation was re-established, and the bulk of the right arm so much increased, that after three weeks, it equalled that of the left arm. In the meantime the urine had, by the use of Vichy water, become quite clear, and the appetite had considerably increased. The interossei and lumbricals were most stubborn, and only showed signs of improvement at the end of the third week. They then rapidly regained power, and when the patient discontinued the treatment, after having been under my care for five weeks, he was in every respect in excellent health, and able to resume his avocation.

CHAPTER III.

PARALYSIS.

31. Paralysis is one of the most frequent and one of the most important affections of the nervous system; and there are few diseases upon which pathological anatomy, experimental physiology, and clinical experience have of late shed so much light, as they have upon paralysis. Not unfrequently investigations into the nature of diseases have been full of interest in a scientific point of view, but have remained devoid of practical value; since they did not give us any indications as to the curative treatment of these disorders. With paralysis, however, the case has been different; and the more our knowledge of the several forms of paralysis has advanced and expanded, the better we have become able to relieve or to cure one of the greatest afflictions, to which the human system is liable.

32. Paralysis is not a disease *sui generis*, but merely a symptom of disease, to which the most various disorders may give rise. By the term "*true paralysis*," I should, however, designate only those forms of loss of motive power which are caused by disease of the brain, the spinal cord, and the motor nerves; while, by the term of *consecutive paralysis*, I understand those forms which are brought about by diseases of the sentient nerves, the muscles and the bones. This distinction will at once be seen to be of great practical importance, as the treatment has to be altogether different for true and for consecutive paralysis. In the latter, the central and the peripheral nervous system may be in its normal condition, and yet motion be impeded or prevented by fracture or softening of the bones, or by destruction of the irritability of the muscles. Thus the orders of volition may in the usual manner be carried to the muscles; yet these latter do not respond, as they are, from one cause or another, unable to do the work assigned to them. On the other hand, more or less complete paralysis may arise consecutively upon certain affections of the sentient or sensory nerves. Thus it is commonly observed that, if

the lower extremities have lost their normal sensibility, the gait is tottering and uncertain; and if the sentient nerves of the face are impaired in their action, the play of the physiognomical muscles may be diminished or cease altogether. Another instance is amaurosis, where the eyes are, as a rule, fixed and staring, although their several movements may still be executed at will. Again, in deaf-and-dumbness, it is only a pair of sentient nerves, which are originally suffering, viz., the auditory nerves; but consequently upon their affection, a more or less complete loss of speech is inevitably entailed. In these latter forms of consecutive paralysis, nothing but the stimulus to motion is wanting, in order to bring about the cessation of the paralysis. Thus, if in amaurosis the optic nerve should regain the power of vision, the fixed and staring position of the eye would disappear; if in a case of anæsthesia of the lower extremities, sensation should be restored, the gait would again become as firm as ever; if in a child which has, by a blow or fall, become deaf, and has, in consequence of the deafness, ceased to talk, we should be able to restore the vital action of the auditory nerves, the consecutive paralysis of speech would gradually disappear without any special treatment, as the organ of speech would then receive its proper stimulus.

33. Quite different from such affections is true paralysis, which is frequently caused by diseases of the centre of volition, especially hæmorrhage into, and rupture of the fibres of, the brain; whereby the normal connection between the brain and the motor nerves is destroyed, so that the orders of the will are no longer transmitted to the muscles, which are therefore incapable of executing voluntary movements. The same may occur if, without any lesion of the continuity of the brain-fibres, the nutrition of this organ is impaired, as, for instance, by the want of proper food, or in the convalescence from certain acute diseases, such as diphtheria, small-pox, typhoid fever, in lead-poisoning; or if there are tumours pressing on the brain, and thus conduction is impeded. In cases of this kind the paralysis may be either confined to certain parts, or it may be general.

34. In diseases of the spinal cord the paralysis extends as far as the disease itself has encroached upon the substance of the cord; all nerves and muscles below the seat of that disease are paralysed, while the nerves above it may be in their normal condition. If there is a disease of the

medulla oblongata, both the upper and lower extremities are paralysed; and, at the same time, respiration and deglutition are impaired or altogether prevented. Finally, if a motor nerve or a plexus of motor nerves is paralysed, by concussion, pressure, inflammation, or other causes, the muscles animated by these nerves are incapable of motion.

35. The degree of paralysis is very variable, and depends upon the changes which have taken place in the nervous centres, motor nerves and muscles. If the polarity of nervous matter has been entirely suppressed, the paralysis is complete; but if it is only diminished, motion is still possible, although it will be feeble and sluggish.

36. As regards the extent of the paralytic affection, there are numerous variations, not only if the paralysing lesion has acted upon peripheral nerves, but also where the centres of the nervous system are affected. In some instances, only a few nerves and muscles are suffering, while in others the disease gradually invades every nerve and muscle of the body, and finally causes death by paralysis of the diaphragm, and other muscles of respiration. If the paralysing lesion has its seat in the brain, the voluntary motive power is annihilated in the whole or part of the opposite side of the body

(*hemiplegia*), this being due to the decussation the fibres.

If both sides of the brain are diseased, bot sides of the body are paralysed, the paralys being most striking in the side opposite to th part of the brain which is mostly affected.] cases where the lower portion of the spinal co suffers, there is paralysis of the lower extremiti (*paraplegia*), and the bladder and rectum suff at the same time.

37. Paralysis invariably exerts a considerab influence upon the state of nutrition, secretio and animal heat in the affected parts. In mo cases of hemiplegia a certain degree of anæsthes is likewise present, and then the blood-vessels a contracted and carry an insufficient supply blood to the organs. In consequence of this, tl temperature of the parts is considerably diminishe and is often not higher than that of the surroun ing air. The pulse is irregular, and weaker the paralysed than in the sound side. The sk of the affected side of the face is flaccid, pale, a loose; the arm and leg are often of a livid colo The epidermis peels off continually, the na grow slowly and are easily split, and perspirati is tardy. Œdema in the lower extremities m

be also present, arising from the pressure to which the paralysed limb is subjected, if kept for some time in an unsuitable position. The actions of sinapisms and blisters is slower than usual; ulcers do not readily heal and decubitus is apt to set in, more especially in paralysis arising from a disease of the spinal cord. In cases of this latter kind, the secretion of urine is generally diminished, and its re-action alkaline instead of acid. The bones are lighter, owing to their insufficient nutrition; the muscles are pale, thin, and flaccid, and often undergo fatty degeneration. On the other hand, in cases where paralysis is accompanied with hyperæsthesia, the blood-vessels are dilated and contain more blood than usual; the temperature is therefore increased, and the whole aspect of the case quite different from that which obtains if anæsthesia is present.

38. The causes of paralysis are exceedingly various. With regard to general disposition, it appears that in young and old persons the brain is more apt to suffer, while in the middle-aged the spinal cord is most frequently affected. On the whole, the male sex is far more exposed to paralysis, than the female, owing, no doubt, to the greater strain upon the nervous system in the more active life of man.

Mechanical injuries of the nervous matter, suc as wounds, fracture, and dislocation of the bon of the skull and of the vertebral column, fr quently cause paralysis. Peripheral paralysis certain motor nerves by mechanical injury is eve more frequent than central paralysis, and is du to pressure by effusions, extravasations, tumour exostoses, tubercle, cancer, echinococcus an aneurism. Curvature of the spine, especially th form of it which is known as cyphosis; and difi cult and protracted labour are also not unfreque mechanical causes of paralysis.

Not every morbid condition of the nervous cer tres is, however, followed by loss of motive powe thus, in inflammation of the surface of the brain an spinal cord the first symptoms are generally hype æsthesia and spasms, and general weakness, whic are only, after a time, succeeded by paralysis. Bu when the thalamus opticus, the corpus striatum, th corpora quadrigemina, the pons Varolii, the cru cerebri and the medulla oblongata suffer, paralys is immediately produced. Tumours may exist considerable time within the cranium, and becom of considerable size before they cause paralysis the loss of power may then appear suddenly, an may afterwards be diminished and increased intervals, until at last, a permanent paralytic condition is produced. Atrophy of the brain, and hydrocephalus, are mostly followed by paralysis, which, in this case, is not only general, but also presently becomes complete. Sclerosis of the brain and the spinal cord is a rare disease, but where it occurs, it almost always causes paralysis.

If, by some impediment to circulation, less blood than is necessary is carried to the nerves, paralysis is the almost immediate result. This occurs after a ligature of, or an embolus in, an artery, or if the arterial tube is closed up by atheromatous and chalky deposits between its coats.

Simple exhaustion of nervous power, by overwork, anxiety, and excesses of every kind, is likewise a frequent cause of paralysis. This latter also occurs in the course of certain convulsive diseases, as epilepsy, chorea, hysteria, and others. Poisoning by narcotic drugs, such as opium, prussic acid, belladonna, etc., and by certain metals, such as arsenic, mercury, and lead, generally entail paralytic conditions.

Certain diseases of the blood, as scrofula, tubercle, and syphilis, are frequent causes of paralysis.

In these instances, it is, however, mostly due to pressure by glandular tumours, and deposit of tubercular matter within the nerves and their sheaths; syphilis acts most frequently by osteo-periostitis, which occurs at the internal surface and the base of the skull. Rheumatism is likewise often accompanied by partial or total loss of power. Finally, I must mention reflex action as a cause, that is, an outside irritation, starting from some sentient nerve, passing to the spinal cord, and thus causing paralysis.

39. The diagnosis of the cause and seat of paralysis is, in many instances, exceedingly difficult, and is as important as it is difficult. The physician must therefore employ every scientific means at his disposal, in order to elucidate these two points as completely and satisfactorily as possible. The patient should be most carefully examined, while sitting still, lying, standing, and walking about. Not only the voluntary, but also the reflex movements, respiration, deglutition, and the state of the sphincters should be carefully investigated. At the same time, the state of sensation must be examined by the æsthesiometer and other means.

40. A most important means of diagnosis in paralytic affections, is the electric current properly

administered. After galvanism had been used for some time in their treatment, it was observed that the muscles, which were no longer under the influence of volition, were, in some instances, readily brought into play by the current, while in other cases no contractions, or only very feeble ones, were produced. Hence it was thought possible to employ galvanism as a means of making or facilitating the diagnosis of these affections. Unfortunately, however, such observations were, in most instances, negligently made, conclusions hastily drawn, and consequently the greatest confusion produced. For example, in August, 1850, a French Physician, M. Martinet, read a paper before the Paris Academy of Medicine, in which he stated that the presence of electro-muscular contractility was the distinctive character of cerebral, hysterical, and rheumatic paralysis; whilst its absence was an indication of disease of the spinal cord. Yet all these assertions are incorrect!

41. Paralysis due to *disease of the brain* may be recognised by loss of power in one side of the body. The face and tongue always take part in the paralysis, but in most cases they quickly recover. The affection is generally more striking

in the upper than in the lower extremity, and the sphincters are scarcely ever affected. Reflex movements usually occur in the paralysed muscles, but if the affection is of long standing, these movements may also become impossible, and there are muscular contractions which, at a later stage of the affection, it is very difficult to cure.

42. To Dr. Marshall Hall the merit is due of having first directed the attention of the profession to the value of electricity in the diagnosis of paralytic diseases. He contended that cerebral and spinal paralysis were in totally opposite conditions in reference to the irritability of the muscular fibre in the limbs severally affected. By cerebral paralysis he understood that which removes the influence of the brain,—paralysis of spontaneous or voluntary motion, such as is produced by disease of the brain itself, or by disease of the dorsal portion of the spinal cord; while by spinal paralysis he understood that which removes the influence of the spinal cord. By this arbitrary distinction, great confusion was produced in the literature on the subject, as most authors identified spinal paralysis with that produced by disease of the spinal cord. Dr. Hall, however,

contended that in cerebral paralysis the paralytic limbs were always moved by an influence lower than that required to affect the healthy limb; or if both limbs were agitated it was uniformly the paralytic limb which was more shaken than the other. In spinal paralysis, on the contrary, the irritability of the muscles was diminished or even annihilated. Therefore he thought galvanism might afford a source of diagnosis between

1. Hemiplegia of the face, and
2. Paralysis of the facial nerve.

3. Hemiplegia of the arm or leg, and
4. Disease of the nerves of these limbs.

5. Disease of the spinal cord in the dorsal region, and
6. Disease of the cauda equina in the lumbar region.

Dr. Hall believed that in cerebral paralysis the irritability of the muscular fibre became augmented from want of the application of the stimulus of volition, the brain being, in his opinion, the exhauster, through its acts of volition, of the muscular irritability, the spinal cord being, on the contrary, the special source of power in the nerves of exciting muscular contraction, and of the irritability of the muscular fibre. In spinal paralysis, therefore, the irritability of the muscular fibre would be diminished, and at length become extinct, in consequence of its source being cut off.

43. An elaborate criticism of Dr. Hall's views has been given by the late Dr. Todd, who refuted the notion of the brain being the exhauster of muscular irritability, by pointing to the physiological fact that the healthy action of a muscle is promoted by exercise within reasonable limits, and that, whatever restricts that exercise, is injurious to the nutrition of the muscle. He afterwards adduced the evidence of thirteen cases of cerebral paralysis, to prove that in certain morbid states of the brain, the contractility or irritability of the muscles of the paralysed limbs is not augmented. Dr. Todd used all kinds of currents in his experiments, viz., the continuous current, the current induced by voltaic electricity, and the magneto-electric current; and he observed that the results of the experiments were not in any way affected by the instrument employed. He observed that in a certain number of cases the paralysed muscles responded very readily to the galvanic stimulus, and even displayed a greater amount of vigour than the muscles of the healthy limbs; and that

in these cases the muscles of the palsied limb always exhibited some degree of rigidity. The vigour of their action in obedience to the galvanic stimulus was proportionate to the amount of rigidity within certain limits. In another class of cases, the stimulus produced little or no contraction; these were generally cases in which the muscles appeared more or less wasted. In a third class of cases he found that, while the paralysis was almost complete, the galvanic stimulus excited equally the muscles of the paralysed and those of the healthy limbs; these were generally cases of apoplexy occurring in persons previously healthy and not advanced in years.

Dr. Todd also observed that the state of the muscles has comparatively little effect in the production of these phenomena; but that the effect of galvanism is due to the state of nervous force in the paralysed limbs. Thus in cases where the stimulus produces little or no contraction, the nervous force is *depressed* in the nerves of the paralytic limb; in cases where the galvanic stimulus excites contractions of a more lively character in the muscles of the paralysed limb than in those of the healthy limb, the nervous force is *exalted;* and in the third class, where there is no perceptible difference between the two, the nervous force is at its *normal* height. He therefore concluded that galvanism may, in cases of hemiplegia, serve as a test to distinguish between an irritant and a depressing lesion of the brain, but not as a means of distinguishing between cerebral and spinal palsy.

Further researches on this subject were undertaken by M. Duchenne de Boulogne, who strongly objected to the mode of experimentation employed by Dr. Marshall Hall, and stated that the only way to arrive at a satisfactory result was to localise the electric current in the tissue of the paralysed muscles. He gave as the result of his experience that the muscular contractility is always normal in cerebral paralysis, and that there is no difference between the muscles of the healthy and of the paralytic limbs. This statement I can only ascribe to the circumstance, that Duchenne has tested the muscular irritability only in a few cases of cerebral paralysis, and that these happened to be such as are described by Dr. Todd in the third class of cases, in which the muscles retain their normal condition.

44. I have tested the muscular irritability in more than a hundred cases of cerebral paralysis, and

have arrived at the following results:—In a certain number of cases the muscles are flaccid, and the contractility is diminished. In another class of cases the contractility is increased, there is early rigidity of the muscles, and an irritative lesion of the brain; in a third class of cases there is no difference to be observed in this respect between the healthy and the paralytic limb. In the cases in which I have tested muscular excitability I have employed both modes of experimentation, viz., sending the current right through the limbs, and localising the current in the tissue of the muscles. Both methods yielded nearly the same results; but by localising the electric current in the muscles, the difference of muscular contractility appeared far more striking.

I shall now relate a few cases, which may serve as representatives of the three classes which are to be distinguished in paralysis resulting from brain disease.

Case 4. *Hemiplegia resulting from apoplexy; muscular contractility diminished.*

R. V., Esq., aged 57, of originally vigorous and plethoric constitution, but now somewhat debilitated by an antiphlogistic treatment; has never had any serious illness, with the exception o pneumonia, from which he soon recovered Six months ago he had an apoplectic attack accompanied with loss of consciousness fo nearly three hours, and with paralysis of th right side of the face, tongue, right arm, an leg. He did not know how this attack wa brought on. He had sometimes suffered fron palpitation of the heart, but the sounds and th volume of the heart were quite normal. He ha not indulged in excesses of any kind; but hi father died from apoplexy. The paralysis of th face soon disappeared, and the muscles of the arn and leg also regained some mobility. He writes however, with a quivering hand, and canno well manage the spoon, fork, and knife; h complains chiefly of his walking being greatl impaired.

His judgment and memory are not in the leas disturbed; no pain in the head nor limbs. Th cheek is not drawn to the side, nor does th tongue deviate from the median line. The move ments of the eyes are quite normal. The speecl is not impaired. The skin of the right arm anc leg is cold and flaccid. Pulse 76, weaker in th right than in the left side. As to the state o sensation, there is a feeling of numbness in the right arm and leg, and they are not so sensitive to the prick of a pin as they ought to be. The muscles of the right arm and leg are relaxed and diminished in bulk. The motion of the extensors is chiefly impaired, while the patient can grasp pretty well. There is not the least rigidity of the muscles, neither in the upper nor in the lower extremity. Passive extensions of the fore-arm upon the arm, and of the leg upon the thigh, may be done without any resistance felt on the part of the muscles. The galvanic stimulus, administered in a moderate dose and with slow intermittences, did not excite any motion in the paralysed extensor muscles of the right arm, while the current of the same intensity and equally slowly interrupted, excited quite distinct motion in the muscles of the left arm.

The diminished state of muscular contractility, together with the other symptoms of the patient, allowed the conclusion that there was no longer any intracranial irritation; and as six months had elapsed since the attack, the cyst was probably formed. As it may be fairly supposed that in such cases not unfrequently the seat of the paralysis is no longer in the brain, but in the muscles which are impaired by the long rest they hav necessarily taken after the attack,—paralysis fro desuetude—I saw no objection to the electr treatment, and applied a moderate and slowly interrupted current, by means of moist spong lodged in metallic cylinders, the electrodes bein held as close as possible to each other. Th nutrition of the muscles was much improved b the treatment, as after sixteen operations the bu of the muscles was increased, the circulation w re-integrated, the heat was the same in bo extremities, and no difference was to be felt in th pulsations of the right and left radial arter Writing as well as walking had become mu easier, although not yet quite so easy as they ha been before the attack.

Case 5. Hemiplegia; irritation of the brain; au mented excitability of the muscles.

In December, 1858, a patient of the name King was under the care of Dr. Todd, in King College Hospital; he had had repeated attacks apoplexy, and probably suffered from a tumo in the brain, which kept up continual irrit tion. The patient at that time had ptosis the left upper eyelid, and paralysis of t right side, with marked rigidity of the flexor muscles. I tested the excitability of the muscles, and found it slightly increased in the paralysed leg, and very much increased in the paralysed arm. When I directed a gentle current to the belly of the extensor communis digitorum of the paralysed fore-arm, a sudden and powerful extension of the fingers took place, which were before firmly closed by rigidity of the flexors; the same current directed to the non-paralysed side did not induce any movements in the fingers, and I had notably to increase the intensity of the current to produce the same amount of contraction as in the paralysed side. As to the direction of the current, I may mention, that the *inverse* current excited somewhat stronger contractions in the paralysed side than the direct; and the *direct* excited somewhat stronger contractions in the sound side than the inverse. These experiments were repeated several times and always with the same result, in the presence of Dr. Todd, Dr. Conway Evans, and a large number of students.

Case 6. Hemiplegia; normal excitability of the muscles.

L. T., aged 62, has long been in a gouty

condition, and had an apoplectic fit seven years ago; in the attack speech and consciousness were lost, and a complete paralysis of the left side had existed for nearly six months, after which time a gradual improvement took place. At present the speech is still impaired, walking is troublesome, and the motion of the left thumb and fore-finger very limited. Although these two fingers have scarcely been used for seven years, the excitability of the extensor and abductor muscles of these fingers is quite normal, as the muscles move freely under the influence of a gentle current. The same was observed in the recti of the thighs.

There is no other form of paralysis except that produced by an irritative lesion of the brain, in which the excitability of the paralysed muscle is exalted. *If, therefore, the muscles of a paralytic limb are, by a current of the same intensity, more powerfully convulsed than those of the sound side, we may fairly conclude that the paralysis is due to brain disease, and that the lesion is of an irritative character.* But the excitability of the muscles is by no means augmented in *all* cases of paralysis resulting from a lesion of the brain; and therefore the distinction established by Dr. Marshall Hall between cerebral and spinal paralysis must be rejected.

45. Besides hemiplegia, there may be paralysis of both sides of the body due to cerebral affections, for instance, if the seat of the disease is in the middle of the Pons or the medulla oblongata. But even in such cases, the affection is mostly not so general as it is if the spinal cord suffers. If the whole of the brain is diseased, as in senile atrophy, and if there are considerable effusions between the meninges, the paralytic symptoms are more indistinct, irregular, and vary a good deal; the speech is then almost always much affected; the nerves of special sense suffer, and so does the intellect.

46. Paralysis from disease of the *spinal cord* may be recognised by the following symptoms:—If the paralysing lesion is seated in the lumbar portion of the cord, there is paralysis of the lower extremities and of the muscles of the pelvis. If the dorsal portion is affected, the abdominal and lumbar muscles suffer likewise, respiration is impeded, there may be tympanitis, priapism and paralysis of the sphincters. Finally, if the cervical portion is diseased, the upper extremities are paralysed, respiration suffers more considerably, and deglutition becomes imperfect; but the intellect and the nerves of special sense remain in

their normal condition. In cases of this kind the excitability of the muscles is diminished in exact ratio to the degree in which their nutrition is impaired; and thus it may at last entirely disappear. Anæsthesia is more complete and permanent in spinal than in cerebral paralysis; the consequence is a more considerable want of nutrition, and great disposition to decubitus. Hemiplegia is very rare as a consequence of disease of the spinal cord; but there is no doubt that it occasionally occurs. In such instances, it is only one-half of the spinal cord that is diseased. The chief sign whereby we may distinguish spinal from cerebral hemiplegia, is the movement of the umbilicus, which, in the former is, by every inspiration, drawn towards the sound side.

47. *Peripheral paralysis* may be recognised by being confined to the course of one or several nerves, in which neither voluntary nor reflex movements occur. If only motor nerves are affected, sensation remains normal; but if mixed nerves suffer, anæsthesia is likewise present. This form of paralysis is frequently preceded by twitches or quiverings in the muscles; it may be caused by a mechanical injury to a nerve, by pressure from tumours, exostoses, etc. In cases of this kind, the

excitability of the muscles is mostly diminished, and may be totally lost.

Case 7. Paralysis of the facial nerve.

S. W., Beverley Ward, St. Mary's Hospital, under the care of Mr. Ure. The history of this case is somewhat obscure, as the patient is deaf in both ears, cannot well read, and her relatives have mentioned very little of her previous state. It appears, however, that her husband on several occasions bruised and otherwise illtreated her, and that once a severe blow was inflicted on the head. The patient complains of head-ache; the muscles of the left side are paralysed, and the prick of a pin is very obtusely felt on the skin of the same side. I applied the electric current locally to the different muscles of the face, but although I used a strong current, scarcely any contractions were to be observed in the paralysed muscles, while those of the right side responded to the galvanic stimulus.

The loss of muscular contractility is in some instances a very valuable guide to diagnosis. Thus Duchenne has recorded a case, in which he noticed loss of the contractility in the paralysed muscles of the shoulder, by which he was led to the diagnosis of local injury to the nerves; and afterwards a syphilitic exostosis was discovered, which compressed certain branches of the cervical and brachial plexus. In most instances, the excitability of the muscles appears to be lost very soon after the lesion of the nerve has occurred.

48. *Hysterical paralysis* only occurs in women, and is usually brought on by terror, anxiety, or excitement. This form generally affects the lower extremities (paraplegia), cases of hysterical hemiplegia being very rare. It may be recognised by the simultaneous presence of other hysterical symptoms, and by the absence of signs indicating a lesion of the centres of the nervous system; moreover this form of paralysis is scarcely ever complete, and the patients are frequently able to move their limbs, when under the influence of emotion, etc. Dr. Todd has already drawn attention to the circumstance that in hysterical paralysis the foot is dragged as a piece of inanimate matter, and that the patients do not endeavour to raise it; while in cerebral hemiplegia the paralysed leg is thrown round by a rotatory movement of the trunk, and is raised by uplifting of the pelvis. According to Duchenne, in all cases of hysterical paralysis the electro-muscular

sensibility (that is, the sensation excited by the electro-muscular contraction) is nearly or totally gone, but the electric excitability of the muscles is normal. In this, however, I cannot agree with him, as I have found that in a certain number of cases of hysterical paralysis—both paraplegia an hemiplegia—the excitability of the muscles is considerably diminished, especially in cases where the affection is of long standing.

Case 8. *Hysterical paraplegia; diminished excitability of the muscles.*

In May, 1858, at the request of Dr. Todd, I faradised a lady, aged 28, unmarried, who, in consequence of a fright, had nearly lost the use of her legs. Her gait was staggering, and when not sufficiently supported the limbs gave way and she fell heavily to the ground. The disease wandered about the limbs, sometimes attacking more the right, at other times more the left, limb; for a short time the right hand also became affected, and writing and playing on the piano became very troublesome. When I first saw her she dragged the right leg as a piece of inanimate matter; the foot swept the ground, and being inclined to turn inside, the inner edge of the shoe was generally torn after it had been used for a very short time only. When sitting, she was scarcely able to raise the foot or to turn it outside, or to move the toes; she experienced very great difficulty in getting up from the sitting posture, as well as in getting into bed at night; and she found it almost impossible to press the pedals of the piano and the harp. On administering a gentle electro-magnetic current to the rectus of the *left* thigh the muscle was immediately seen to contract; but the same current proved utterly incapable of moving the rectus of the *right* thigh, and although I notably increased the intensity of the current, whereby a strong sensation was produced, only feeble vibrations appeared in the fibres of the right rectus. The same state was observed in the peronei and tibiales muscles; and it was only after sixteen operations; that the nutrition was so far restored that all the muscles of the right limb were equally affected by the electric current as were those of the left.

LEAD-PALSY.

49. Lead gets into the blood either by inhaling it through the lungs, as is done, for instance, by persons sleeping in newly-painted rooms, or it

may become absorbed by the skin. In other instances, it is taken with the food, especially in adulterated wine and beer; and recently many cases have been recorded in which the lead passed into the blood of the patients, by their taking snuff which had been packed in lead-foil. The paralysis, which is the consequence of lead-poisoning, always affects certain sets of muscles, leaving others nearly or totally intact. The arms are almost always affected, while the lower extremities remain comparatively free from the disease; in the arm, the flexor muscles are mostly spared and the extensors are attacked. Generally the extensor communis digitorum is the first which becomes affected; afterwards the extensors of the fore-finger and of the little finger begin to suffer; and lastly, the extensors carpi radialis and ulnaris, the triceps and deltoid, and the muscles of the ball of the thumb are affected. In cases of this kind the excitability of the muscles is always much diminished, and often entirely lost; such is the case not only when atrophy has been the consequence of lead-poisoning, but also when the bulk of the muscles is only slightly diminished; and the excitability of the muscles, in certain instances, remains still impaired after the voluntary movements have regained their former power.

It is generally easy to recognise paralysis from lead-poisoning, since the blue line on the gums, the constipation, colics, and the different forms of neuralgia and spasms, which are mostly present, serve to facilitate the diagnosis.

Case 9. *Lead-palsy; excitability of the muscles gone.*

Samuel R—, painter, aged 28. He has had several attacks of lead-colic, from which he recovered under medical care. Six weeks before I saw him, he had pain in the joints, and cramps in the legs. He now complains of the dropping of the left hand, also of obstinate constipation. A blue line on the gums is distinctly visible. All the extensor muscles of the left fore-arm, as well as the deltoid, are paralysed; the left arm and the fingers cannot be lifted. But if the first phalanges are supported, the patient can extend the second and third phalanges; which proves that the interossei and lumbricals have not suffered. The back of the fore-arm is concave by atrophy of the extensors. The raising of the arm is difficult, and the extending to a right angle with the body is impossible. The flexor muscles are not affected. The right arm is weak, but not paralysed. The lower extremities are not impaired. On applying a strong current to the deltoid muscle, only a little tremulousness appears in its fibres, which are wasted, and in the extensors on the back of the fore-arm no contraction was to be produced. I faradised the patient every other day, for about four weeks, after which he regained much more strength in the muscles, the volume of which had considerably increased; still the excitability of the extensors of the left arm was less than that of those of the right.

To prove the value of galvanism as a means of diagnosis in cases of this kind, I may here add another case of paralysis of the fore-arm, which was not caused by lead-poisoning.

Case 10. *Spontaneous paralysis of the extensors on the back of the fore-arm; excitability normal.*

W. W., out-patient of St. Mary's Hospital, was sent to me by Mr. Edwards. Without any premonitory symptoms having been observable, the patient, about a fortnight before I saw him, found, on awaking in the morning, that he could not move the right arm; the hand drops, the lateral movements of it are also lost, and the sensibility of the skin on the back of the fore-arm is impaired, Neither lead-poisoning, nor concussion of the radial or ulnar nerve, rheumatism, disease of the brain, fatty degeneration, nor atrophy of the muscles, is present. No pain, but numbness is complained of, and all the extensor muscles excited by the lower branches of the radial nerve have lost their energy. The excitability of these muscles is not at all impaired, but scarcely any sensation is produced by the electro-muscular contraction. When I directed the electric current to the paralysed muscles of this patient, he felt them move, but although I applied the most rapid intermittences of a very strong current, not the least pain was felt, while the same current applied to the healthy muscles of the left fore-arm produced an extremely disagreeable and almost tetanic sensation. I ought not to omit mentioning that, for acquiring an exact knowledge of the state of this sensation, it will not do to compare the sensibility in the paralysed extensors with that of the healthy flexors of the same fore-arm, as the skin on the anterior side of the fore-arm is much more delicate, and therefore offers much less resistance to the passage of the current than the skin on the back of the fore-arm. Therefore, in experiments of this kind, only the corresponding muscles of the right and of the left side are to be compared.

The difference in the general aspect of the cases 9 and 10 may be easily observed. But the symptoms of the effects of lead upon the system are not always so distinct as in case 9; indeed, sometimes the dropping of the wrist is the first symptom of the lead-poisoning. The diagnosis, however, between lead-palsy and cases like 10, has not only a theoretical but also a practical interest, as in lead-palsy the application of electricity must be combined with a general treatment, while local palsies, without structural changes, generally soon disappear when treated by Faradisation only. When a patient states that he has never been exposed in business to the injurious influences of lead, we cannot therefore conclude that the paralysis is not caused by lead-poisoning; as lead is often administered to the system for a length of time in adulterated food and drink without the patient's having the least knowledge of it. Nor is the paralysis of the extensor muscles always preceded by, or simultaneous with, symptoms which belong to the constitutional disease, and will, if observed, facilitate the diagnosis. Only the relation of the muscles to the Faradic stimulus helps, in doubtful cases, to establish the diagnosis, as the excitability of the muscles is always either lost or diminished in lead-palsy, whilst it is normal in spontaneous paralysis. *Therefore when the muscles of a paralytic limb move well under the influence of the electric current, we may fairly conclude that there is no lead in the system.*

50. *Rheumatic paralysis* is not difficult to recognise, as there are always other symptoms present indicating the existence of the rheumatic poison in the blood. In this form of paralysis, the electro-muscular contractility is, according to Duchenne, quite normal, while the sensation excited by the electro-muscular contraction may be even stronger on the suffering side than in the healthy parts. This is true for recent cases; but in cases of long standing, I have almost invariably found the excitability of the muscles impaired.

WASTING PALSY.

51. The excitability of the muscles is, in this disease, quite proportional to the more or less atrophic state of the muscular fibres. The more the bulk

of the muscle is diminished, the weaker is the contraction exhibited by it. In this disease, electricity enables us to distinguish the state of almost every muscle and bundle of a muscle, whether normal or atrophied. Thus, for instance, I have seen cases in which the whole substance of the extensor communis digitorum was not atrophied, but merely that portion of the muscle which extends the middle finger. This was easily distinguished by placing the electrodes of an induction apparatus upon the belly of the extensor communis, when only the fore-finger, the fourth, and the little finger were extended, while the middle finger remained quite or nearly motionless. The same is often to be observed if we faradise the interossei and lumbricals, when only one or two of the muscles will respond to the electric current, while the remaining ones are not affected, unless a very strong current be used.

52. We have thus arrived at the result, that the muscles of paralysed limbs may present three different conditions when subjected to the action of the electric current, and that this may enable us, in certain cases, to form the diagnosis of the paralysing lesion.

a. If the excitability of the muscles—or rather

the polarity of the motor nerves—be *increased* in the paralysed limb, the case is one of *cerebral paralysis*, connected with an irritative lesion within the cranium.

b. If the excitability of the muscles be nearly or totally *lost*, we have, in all probability, either *lead-palsy* or *traumatic paralysis;* but it must be kept in mind, that certain hysterical and rheumatic palsies of long-standing present the same peculiarity; and that it also may be found in cases of disease of the brain and the cord.

c. If paralysed muscles respond readily to the electric current, there is no lead in the system, nor is there any lesion of continuity in the motor nerves; but if such cases are of *long standing*, they are due to *brain disease;* and if they are of *recent standing*, they are generally instances of *hysterical*, *rheumatic*, or *spontaneous* paralysis.

53. The *prognosis* is very different according to the cause of the affection. If the paralysis be occasioned by a cancer or tubercle invading the nervous matter, it is exceedingly unfavourable. Inflammation, extravasation, extensive softening and atrophy of the brain are likewise apt to cause permanent paralysis; but where there is merely pressure from without, as by effusion or extravasa-

tion in the meninges, a cure may be brought about if absorption of the effusion or extravasation be induced. In disease of the vertebral column, in obliteration of the arteries, in tumours pressing upon peripheral nerves, a cure may likewise take place. If the paralysis is caused by poisoning with mercury, lead, or syphilis, the prognosis is mostly favourable, unless the cases should be very far advanced; and the same may be said of rheumatic and hysterical paralysis. If a mechanical injury to a nerve has caused paralysis, a regeneration of the nervous substance may take place, and thus the affection may completely disappear. Paralysis arising from disease of the spinal cord is scarcely ever entirely cured; but even in this affection, by the employment of suitable remedies, great relief and improvement may be produced.

54. The *treatment* of paralysis must vary according to the causes of the affection, the symptoms that may be present, and the constitution of the patient. The chief consideration must always be whether the cause is still acting, or whether the pathological process to which the affection was due, has run its course. In the former case, we must endeavour to remove the cause, in the latter, a symptomatic treatment is of principal importance.

The remedies to be used in the treatment of paralysis, are both internal and external. Amongst the former, arnica has been very much employed, especially where the paralysis is due to pressure; but there is no doubt that in most cases of paralysis arnica produces only little benefit. M. Trousseau has lately recommended large doses of rhus radicans in paraplegia due to exhaustion, but experience has not justified his expectations. In paraplegia due to myelitis, ergot of rye and and belladonna should be used. If there are exudations in the meninges, iodide of potassium frequently proves beneficial. Strychnine and brucine should not be employed in cases of paraplegia where there is irritation or inflammation, but only where the affection is due to white softening or to reflex action. In paraplegia of syphilitic origin, iodide of potassium or bichloride of mercury frequently effect a cure. Phosphorus, sulphur, ammonia, iron, quinine, and cod-liver oil, are useful in certain conditions which will be mentioned hereafter.

Where reflex movements are to be caused, the mucous membranes should be stimulated, by emetics, purgatives, enemata, diuretics, smelling salts and sneezing powders, injections of cold water into the rectum, the bladder, and the vagina. Affusions of cold water and hot applications to the skin, are also useful under these circumstances.

External remedies are of the greatest value in all cases of paralysis, and in some even more directly useful than medicines internally administered. Cold baths, shower-baths, the hot and cold douche, the spas of Gastein, Wildbad, Pfäffers, Töplitz, Warmbrunn, and others, the moor and mud-baths which are given in Marienbad and Franzensbad, the pine-leaf baths, which are chiefly used in special establishments in Saxony and Hanover, shampooing, rubbing, the cold water cure, used with moderation, are, in many cases, of great benefit. It requires, however, great discrimination on the part of the Physician to prescribe these several remedies, as they may, in certain conditions, do harm, more especially where there is great irritation. Where paraplegia is due to a disease of the vertebral column, the moxa is an excellent remedy.

55. The best stimulus for the motor nerves and muscles is unquestionably the electric current properly administered, and there is scarcely any form of paralysis in which it may not be employed

with more or less decided benefit to the patien I shall therefore describe the physiological an curative action of the electric current at som length.

If a living motor nerve be subjected to th action of a continuous galvanic current, contrac tions of all the muscles animated by this nerv are produced, on closing as well as on openin the circuit, whether the current be direct c inverse.

The contractions produced by the entrance an the cessation of the current do however not tak place in consequence of the motor nerve simpl conducting the electric fluid to the muscles; fc if a wet thread be tightly applied to a nerve, s that it becomes thin and reduced to its neur lemma, we shall never succeed in exciting cor tractions in the muscles animated by this nerv if the electrodes be applied to the nerve above th point where it has been tied; although by such proceeding the propagation of electricity is nc interrupted, the wet thread conducting equall well as the nerve. Another still more remarkab instance is, that a few drops of ether applied any point of the nerve, will suspend the contrac tions of the muscles, if the electrodes be place above or at the point where the ether has been applied; the contractions, however, will re-appear as soon as the effects of ether have passed off. Finally, if we galvanise the nerves of a frog which has previously been poisoned by woorara, not the least contraction will occur in the muscles animated by these nerves; although woorara does in no way affect the electric conductility of the nerves, which remains perfectly intact; nor the contractile power of the muscles, for the muscles are seen to suffer commotions if an electric current is directly applied to them without the intervention of the nerves; it is only because woorara destroys that peculiar force by which the nerves are enabled to produce the play of the muscles. The electric current excites the nerve and puts in action its power of producing muscular contractions; it causes a disturbance in the molecular equilibrium of the nerve, whereby the nerve is enabled to bring about a shortening of the muscular fibres attended by an increase in their diameter.

56. During the time that a continuous galvanic current traverses a motor nerve, no visible effect takes place in the muscles, providing the current of the battery is constant. Indeed, the remark-

able physiological effects occur at the moment when the density of the current suddenly rises from zero to a certain height, as is the case on establishing the circuit; and, on the other hand, when the density of the current descends again from a certain height to zero, as is the case on breaking the circuit. Proceeding from these facts, Du Bois Reymond has arrived at an electro-physiological law for the motor nerves, which he has proposed in the following terms:—"The motor nerve is not excited by the absolute amount of the density of the current, but merely by the variations which occur in the density of the current from one instant to the other; and the physiological effect is the greater, the more considerable are the variations of the density of the current; that is, in proportion as they take place more rapidly, or as they are more considerable in a given space of time." It is obvious that this affords a striking analogy to the development of induction-currents in coils of wires connected with the poles of a battery; as induction-currents are only produced on making and breaking the circuit of the battery, but not while the circuit is closed.

By Du Bois Reymond's law it is easy to explain

a number of phenomena which had been observed a long time ago. Thus, for producing contractions it is not absolutely necessary that the current traversing a nerve should be closed or opened, as thereby only the maximum of variation is produced. Physiological effects will also be brought about by minor variations in the density of the current; for instance, if the intensity of the current traversing a motor nerve be suddenly increased; or if another current be suddenly brought to bear upon a nerve traversed by a continuous current; or if a portion of the current traversing a nerve be suddenly diverted. Since variations of this kind are not so considerable, the physiological effects, therefore, will not be so striking, as those observed on closing or opening the circuit.

It is also easy to understand from Du Bois Reymond's law the action of an induced current upon the nerves and muscles. Induction currents are instantaneous, they consist only of great and sudden variations, which succeed each other more or less rapidly, in consequence of the commencement and the cessation of the current of the battery, and the magnetisation and demagnetisation of the soft iron. A single induced current will act just as does the opening or closing the circuit of the battery; there will be a contraction produced by the disturbance of the molecular equilibrium of the nerve; but the muscle will immediately be relaxed again. But when the induction currents succeed each other rapidly, the contractions caused by them will likewise take place in rapid succession, and the muscle will relax less and less the more rapidly the intermittences be given. In a certain rapidity of the intermittences the contraction will appear continuous, as if produced by the will; this apparently continuous contraction, however, consists only of a very rapid succession of single contractions, the intervals between which are too short to be distinguished. The induction apparatus which I usually employ can furnish 120 currents in a second; so that if it be applied to a muscle, 120 single contractions may be produced in a second, and 7,200 in a minute. This circumstance furnishes a clue to understand why the induced current is a more powerful remedy for paralytic affections than the continuous current.

57. Although it is especially the *variations* occurring in the density of the current which are of influence in the production of contractions, the

intensity and the *direction* of the exciting current are also of great importance.

If a feeble continuous current be applied to a nerve, the nerve will retain its excitability very long, and will not be destroyed, as is done by mechanical and chemical stimuli. But if the continuous current be of a certain intensity (if instead of a single battery a pile be applied), the nerve may be destroyed, both by the calorific and the chemical action of the pile, especially at the point where the negative pole has touched the nerve. If a nerve to which an intense continuous current has been applied, be afterwards subjected again to the action of a feeble continuous current or an induced current, above or at the point where the negative pole has been applied, no physiological effect whatever is produced; but if the same nerve be excited at a point near to the muscle and beneath the negative pole, a contraction of the muscles animated by it will again be produced. It is only the continuous galvanic current which is capable of destroying a nerve by its calorific and chemical action; if the continuous current be constantly interrupted and re-established again by means of a cut-current or rheotome; or if, instead of the continuous current, induction currents are employed, a destruction of the nerve will not be caused.

58. The phenomena produced by the electric excitation of motor nerves will also present certain differences according to the *direction* of the current; but as I have shown, on a former occasion,* that they have not that important physiological bearing which had been attributed to them by previous observers, I do not think it necessary to go into any detail respecting them, and proceed to consider the important question, if there be any physiological effect produced during the time that a closed continuous current traverses a nerve?

The first who directed his attention to this subject was Ritter, who observed that if a frog's leg be traversed for a certain time, say half an hour, by a direct continuous current, it will no longer exhibit any contractions, if the current be interrupted and afterwards established and broken again; but that it will suffer a commotion if an inverse current be applied to the nerve: this commotion is feeble on making the circuit, and strong on breaking it. If now an inverse current be made to act upon a leg, its excitability will be in-

* See my "Treatise on Medical Electricity," p. 110.

creased. Hence Ritter concluded that the direct current exercises a paralysing action on the nerve, while the inverse current would augment its irritability.

A few years afterwards Volta made some experiments to determine the effect of the closed circuit of the pile upon the motor nerves. While Ritter had operated with a single galvanic pair, Volta employed the pile, that is, a much stronger current, and therefore obtained different results, which may be described as follows: Both the direct and inverse current exercise a paralysing action when they have traversed the nerve for a certain time. When the nerve has been subjected to the action of a direct current, the frog's limb does no more respond to the excitation of the same; but it will be convulsed anew if an inverse current be substituted to the direct, and *vice versâ*. These processes may be repeated several times, and we may thus annihilate and revive *ad libitum* the readiness of the muscles to respond to the galvanic current. The succession of phenomena just described has been designated by the name of *voltaic alternatives*; but to Ritter the merit is due of having first proved that the closed continuous current has a distinct action upon the motor nerve.

Volta's researches upon the action of the closed circuit were at a later period repeated by Marianini, who operated with a pile consisting of sixty pairs of plates, and confirmed Volta's results. Nobili tried to explain these phenomena in the following way: He assumed three different states in the nerve—*a.* the natural state; *b.* the state of direct alteration, brought about by a prolonged action of a direct continuous current upon a nerve; and *c.* the state of inverse alteration produced by the passage of the inverse current. In order that there should be a commotion in the muscles, there must be a sudden transition in the nerve from one state to the other; and by the prolonged action of a continuous current, whatever may be its direction, the nerve is rendered incapable of transmitting the action of a current moving in the same direction; it only gains back this property if it be allowed to rest for a certain time, or if it be acted upon by a current guided in a contrary direction. But although in general the frog may contract anew, yet its excitability will be found to be diminished, and by repeated applications the excitability of the nerve will at last be entirely destroyed.

59. Thus it appears that the excitability of the nerve is diminished by a prolonged action of a

continuous current of a certain intensity upon the nerve. We may, therefore, ask: is a continuous current capable of paralysing the action of any stimulus applied to the nerve, or of any irritated state of a nerve produced by any means whatever; and is it indifferent in what direction the current is made to pass through the nerve in order to produce the said paralysing action?

That a continuous current may, under certain circumstances, quiet an irritated state of a nerve, had already been observed by Nobili, who remarked now and then in the course of his experiments, that prepared frogs became subjected to violent tetanus without any apparent cause; and that these frogs became quiet if a continuous current was sent through their limbs in a certain direction, while the tetanus remained undisturbed if the current moved in the contrary direction. Matteucci afterwards observed that when frogs, tetanised by strychnia, were subjected to the action of a continuous galvanic current, the tetanus disappeared very soon, and did not come back; the frogs died from the effects of strychnia, but without the convulsions which are otherwise the consequence of strychnia poisoning. As to the direction of the current, he stated that tetanus would cease by the passage of an inverse current, while it would be increased by the direct current. Together with M. Farina, he tested even the therapeutical effect of the continuous current in a patient who suffered from traumatic tetanus in consequence of having been shot through the leg. He caused a current of thirty to forty pairs of plates to pass along the spinal marrow in the direction from the sacrum to the nape of the neck, and introduced the patient gradually into the circuit in order to avoid muscular commotions. The patient opened his mouth, the circulation and transpiration was re-established, and the patient appeared generally comforted, but died nevertheless afterwards, the irritation having been kept up by foreign bodies in the wounded limb.

Another instance has been mentioned by Du Bois-Reymond, who remarked that in a tetanised limb of a frog the gastrocnemian muscle became quiet as soon as the sciatic nerve was laid upon the tendon of the muscle; that is, if the *inverse* current proper of the muscle was made to pass through the nerve; but that the tetanus continued unchanged, when the nerve touched the flesh of the muscle, that is, when the *direct* current proper of the muscle traversed the nerve.

60. The most important researches, however, bearing upon this question, have recently been undertaken by Professor Eckhard, of Giessen, who was led to the conclusion that if a constant continuous current of a certain intensity and direction be made to pass through a nerve, the excitability of this nerve will be so much diminished that any mechanical, chemical, or electrical stimulus, which would otherwise bring about a contraction of the muscle, will no longer be able to induce such contractions, so long as the galvanic current continues to traverse the nerve; but that as soon as the circuit has been opened again, contractions will be brought about if the nerve be excited anyhow.

In order to ascertain the difference in the action of a direct and of an inverse current, Professor Eckard has made three series of experiments, with two pairs of Daniell's battery.

I. He placed the positive electrode at a certain point of the nerve, and the negative lower down; he then tetanised the muscles by applying some salt water to the nerve, at a point *between* the two electrodes; as soon as the electrodes had been connected with the poles of the battery, that is, a direct continuous current traversed the irritated nerve, the tetanus disappeared; whe the circuit was opened again, the tetanic coı vulsions set in as before. The paralysing effe was more striking if, instead of the direct, tl inverse current traversed the nerve; the inver current of the same intensity being able t counterbalance a stronger stimulus, the actio of which was only slightly diminished by tl direct current.

II. The continuous current was made to pa through a motor nerve, as above, and afterwards stimulus applied, not between, but *above* the ele trodes. The result was the same as in I.; bot the direct and the inverse current exercised paralysing action, but that of the inverse was moı remarkable than that of the direct. If, instead a mechanical or chemical stimulus, an induce current was used to excite the nerve, the paralysir effect was strongest, if both the continuous ar the induced current moved upwards.

III. An inverse continuous current was seı through a nerve, and the stimulus no more applie between or above, but *beneath* the electrodes; tl paralysing effect was again observed, whether sa water or the induced current were used as e: citants. Then a direct continuous current w made to pass through the nerve, and the curio fact observed that in this instance the continuous current did not only exercise no paralysing effect at all, but that, on the contrary, the excitability of the nerve was increased by its passage. Tetanus, brought about by the application of salt water to a nerve, became much stronger as soon as the electrodes of a direct continuous current were placed above the excited point. It was even observed that if a nerve had been immersed in salt water, and the tetanus had not yet made its appearance, it came on immediately after the circuit had been established in the way described. If two shocks of an induction apparatus were applied to the nerve, one before the commencement of the continuous current, and another one after the circuit had been established, the contraction produced by the second shock was stronger than that by the first. Hence it results that an inverse continuous current of a certain intensity, when traversing a motor nerve, will enfeeble its excitability altogether, whatever may be the point of the nerve to which the stimulus may have been applied, and whatever may be the nature of the stimulus itself; while a direct continuous current, when passing through a motor nerve, will diminish its excitability only at those points to which the electrodes themselves are applied, and in all point beyond the positive pole; but that it tends t increase the excitability of the nerve on all thos points which are beneath the negative electrod Thus, if the last case did not form an exceptio the continuous current might be fairly termed th paralysing current.

61. A few other instances of the paralysing actio of the continuous current may be given. It well known that the vagi do not form the mot system of the heart, but that they regulate th movements of the heart which are only caused b sympathetic fibres; therefore, if the vagi l excited, the pulsations of the heart are retarde and finally brought to a stand-still. This is th case if an induced current be applied to the vag Very quick pulsations of the heart indicate paralytic state of the vagi, or a state approachin paralysis; thus the pulsations of the heart becon innumerable, if a section of the vagi has bee made. Nearly the same is observed if the va be subjected to the action of a continuous cu rent; namely, a great acceleration of the puls tions of the heart.

Similar phenomena are observed in the lymp hearts of frogs and other reptiles, the pulsatio of which depend upon the nerves which arise from the spinal cord, and thence go to the lymph-hearts. If a section of these nerves have been made, the movements of the lymph-hearts disappear. They may re-appear some time afterwards, but then they will present quite another type of contractions, since only some parts of the lymph-hearts will contract; or if, what is of rare occurrence, the whole heart be seen to contract, the rhythm is wanting which had been apparent before the section of the nerves had been made. On the other hand, a single shock from an induction apparatus produces systole of the lymph-hearts; and, if a succession of induced currents be applied to them, the maximum of contraction is produced, viz., a stand-still of the lymph-hearts during systole, while, if a continuous current be made to pass through the nerves, a paralytic stand-still of the lymph-hearts during diastole will be brought about.

62. As the experiments of Professor Eckhard on the action of the closed continuous current upon the motor nerves have only been made on frogs' limbs separated from the body, I have been anxious to inquire if the same results would be obtained on a nerve still connected with the

nervous centres. In order to ascertain this, the crural nerve of a living rabbit was laid bare, and the continuous current of three large plates of Daniell's battery applied to it. The contraction was obtained, as in Bernard's experiment, only on closing the circuit, whatever was the direction of the current. After the contraction produced by making the circuit had passed off, I applied a stimulus to the nerve which was traversed by the continuous current; viz., an induced current which had been made feeble by the interposition of a layer of water into the circuit The result of this experiment was that the continuous current always proved paralysing, whether the stimulus was applied between, above, or below the electrodes, and whether the current was direct or inverse. The shock from the induction apparatus produced a most marked contraction, when the nerve was not traversed by the continuous current; but as soon as the circuit was closed, the induced current failed to bring about a contraction.

63. The action of the closed continuous current upon the motor nerves is, however, widely different according to the more or less considerable intensity of the current. We have been lately

favoured with some interesting physiological researches on the action of a very powerful continuous current upon the motor nerves, by Dr. Remak, of Berlin, who has come to the following results:—

A current produced by thirty plates of Daniell's battery was sent through the trunks of nerves, and some time afterwards contractions were observed in the antagonistic muscles. Thus, for instance, when he acted upon his own median nerve, he felt a sort of tingling in all the parts animated by branches of the median nerve, and observed a contraction, which gradually increased, in the antagonistic muscles, viz., in the extensors of the wrist and of the fingers. The hand was elevated to an angle of about 45°, and the fingers were extended. This contraction was kept up as long as the current of the battery continued to circulate in the median nerve, but the hand immediately dropped on breaking the circuit. He states besides that he was able to resist the involuntary extension of the hand while the circuit was closed, as he preserved the full force of volition over the muscles animated by the median nerve, but as soon as he ceased to resist, the extension of the wrist and the fingers was again produced. He observed the same if he sent a continuous current through the trunk of the radial nerve, by placing one electrode to the point between biceps and triceps, where the radial nerve may be reached, and the other electrode on the back of the fore-arm, where the interosseous nerve is superficial. He then perceived tonic contractions of the muscles animated by the median and ulnar nerves, that is to say, flexion of the hand and the fingers. These contractions are termed by him, galvano-tonic contractions; to produce them, a current of enormous intensity is always necessary. Usually this current is very painful to bear, and in some instances it may even excite great pain without producing any galvano-tonic contractions at all, while in other instances less pain may be experienced, and the contraction will be well marked. If a certain length of the nervous trunk be traversed by the current, the contractions will be more easily produced than if only a small part of the nerve is acted upon. In some cases it is sufficient to employ twenty to thirty plates of Daniell's battery; in other instances, however, fifty are necessary. Besides, in the same individual the phenomena may be different on different days; viz. at first, contractions of the muscles animated by branches of the nerve which is traversed by the current, and at another time contraction of the antagonistic muscles; sometimes even a struggle may be observed between the different groups of muscles, so that at first a flexion may be produced, and some time afterwards extension, while the current continues to traverse the same nerve. In his opinion these contractions are not produced by the direct excitation of the nerves, but they are reflex movements caused by the excitation of the nervous centres.

64. The experiments which have been made with the Indian arrow-poison woorara, especially by Bernard, Kölliker and myself, have shewn that the muscle may continue to live even if the nerve is dead, and that *by the electric current the molecular equilibrium of the muscles may be directly disturbed, just as well as the molecular equilibrium of the nerves.* As soon as the equilibrium of either motor nerves or muscles is disturbed, contractions are observed. The contractions produced by applying the electric current directly to the contractile tissue of the muscles, present, however, certain peculiarities which are worth noticing.

If the current be directed to a motor nerve, the whole substance of all the muscles which are animated by the nerve enters into contraction; but if the current be directly applied to a muscle only those fibres are seen to contract which are traversed by the current; and if we wish to produce a contraction of the whole substance of a muscle, the electrodes must be placed, one at the upper and the other at the lower end of the muscle. Besides a current of greater intensity is required if we wish to produce muscular contractions without the intervention of nervous filaments, than is necessary if we cause contractions by excitation of the motor nerves. *Hence we may conclude that the molecular equilibrium of the motor nerves is more easily disturbed by the electric current than the molecular equilibrium of the muscles.*

If a muscle is caused to contract by placing the electrodes upon the belly of the muscle, the contraction is composed of two elements; viz. contraction by direct excitation of the muscles, and contraction by excitation of the nervous filaments which are mixed up with the muscles. It is evident that muscular contractions will be most easily produced if such points are touched by the electrodes where the motor filaments are superficial;

but if a sufficiently strong current be employed, contractions will be induced, even if the electrodes are placed on such points of the surface of the muscle, where dissection does not show the exisence of motor filaments.

65. Many interesting facts have been evolved from the application of electricity to the study of the functions of the muscles of the living body; and it has thus become possible to create a kind of living anatomy. Dr. Duchenne of Paris, first undertook systematic researches of this kind, which have led to several important discoveries.

It is true that the deep strata of the muscles, covered by the superficial ones, will not clearly exhibit their contraction. But here, pathology has seconded physiology. It is chiefly muscular atrophy which, by destroying the superficial muscles, takes away the impediments to the passage of the electric current, and thus helps to the knowledge of the function of every muscle of the living body. Many of the theories on the functions of the muscles formerly adopted have thereby fallen to the ground. As one of the most remarkable facts now established, I may mention that the muscle extensor communis digitorum has no influence whatever on the extension of the second and third phalanges, but only on the first, and that it is, in fact, the little interossei and lumbricals that extend the second and third phalanges and bend the first. Also that the muscles flexor sublimis and profundus bend the second and third phalanges, but not the first. This is confirmed by many pathological facts, chiefly in lead-palsy and muscular atrophy. In lead-palsy the extensor digitorum is paralysed, but not the lumbricals and interossei. Therefore, in lead-palsy, the power of extension of the second and third phalanges remains in all its integrity; and only the first phalanges cannot be extended. On the other hand, when the extensor digitorum is not at all paralysed, the hand has sometimes the form of a claw, the interosseous spaces are deeply hollowed, the hand is very thin, the first phalanges are extended, but the second and third are bent. This condition of the hand is due to paralysis and atrophy of the lumbricals and the interossei, and is often cured by the local application of the electric current to the afore-named muscles.

66. Dr. Duchenne has given special study to the function of the muscles of the face, in order to arrive at a knowledge of the mechanism of physiognomical expressions; for it is only the muscles

which are put in action by thoughts, passions, and character; they preserve during muscular repose, the predominance of tonic force, and stamp on every physiognomy its peculiar impression. If there was not in every face this tonic predominance of one or other muscle, all physiognomies would be nearly alike, as the muscles have the same direction, insertion, and strength, and the bones only differ from each other in volume. It is true that, although the facial muscles have only a very small surface, electricity can be localised in each one singly, so as to produce isolated contractions. The way to show most clearly the part every muscle takes in the different physiognomical expressions, is, however, to electrify the muscles of the face of a man just dead, and whose muscles yet retain their excitability; for the living man, when electrified, always mixes involuntary movements with the contraction of the electrified muscle; an impediment, of course, to the observation of the individual action of the muscles.

The frontal muscle, when slightly contracted, cheers up the face; when more contracted, it expresses doubt, surprise; and, when in the highest degree of contraction and united with other muscles, it gives the expression of an agreeable surprise or of terror; it also wrinkles the forehead, and when it is paralysed the wrinkles disappear.

The pyramidales nasi, which are in intimate relation with the frontal muscle, and therefore considered by many anatomists as identical with it, are nevertheless the antagonist of the frontal muscle; they give a sad expression, and, when more contracted, a threatening one. It forms a striking contrast to see these two opposite movements produced in so small a space as the level of the eyebrows.

Isolated contraction of the *orbicularis palpebrarum* and *corrugator supercilii* expresses reflection; and when united to the pyramidalis, they express malice. *The platysma myoides* gives an expression of pain; united with the frontal muscle, it expresses terror; and, with the pyramidalis, rage. Contraction of the *triangularis nasi* gives the expression of lust. The *zygomaticus major* always expresses mirth from simple smiling to the most extravagant hilarity; united with the frontalis, it gives the expression of an agreeable surprise: with the *platysma myoides*, the sardonic laugh: the *zygomaticus minor*, on the contrary, gives a melancholy air. The *levator alæ nasi*, and *labii superioris*, is the real weeping muscle of children, and produces a very ugly grimace. By the contraction of the external fibres of the *orbicularis oris*, the lips are protruded, as for kissing and whistling; the internal fibres press the lips against the teeth, as is done, for instance, by players of the clarionet, for pinching the reed of their instrument between the lips. The *levator menti* is the only muscle in action in persons who repeat their prayers inaudibly, as is often seen in Catholic churches. The *triangularis oris* expresses sadness; in children it is the precursor of tears; in the maximum of its contraction it expresses disgust.

67. The *deltoid* muscle, when galvanised, abducts the humerus, but does not elevate it above the horizontal line. If the anterior fibres only are galvanised, the arm is at once elevated and directed forwards and inwards; if the middle fibres are galvanised, the arm is directed outwards; while, by galvanisation of its posterior fibres, the arm is carried backwards, and the hand raised behind the back. The deltoid muscle is very frequently attacked by wasting palsy.

If the inferior portion of the *trapezius* be galvanised, the base of the scapula is approached to the spinous processes, and the inferior angle of the scapula drawn downwards; this portion tends by its tonic contractility to keep the base of the scapula at a distance of about 2½ inches from the median line. If the *middle portion* of the trapezius be galvanised, the scapula is elevated, and its inferior angle removed from the median line. Finally, if we galvanise the *clavicular portion* of the trapezius, the head is drawn towards the side acted upon and a little backwards, so that the chin is turned towards the opposite side; at the same time the clavicle is raised. If the clavicular portions of both trapezii receive the electric stimulus, the head is reversed backwards. The clavicular portion of the trapezius is very excitable, as it gets nervous fibres from two sources, viz. from the spinal accessory, and from the cervical plexus.

The *latissimus dorsi*, when galvanised, draws the arm downwards and backwards; the scapula is at the same time approached to the median line, but it is not raised.

The *rhomboid muscle* is only accessible to the electric current if the trapezius is destroyed. If it be then galvanised, the scapula is raised; at the same time it is so turned that the inferior angle is nearly in the same line with the external angle. The rhomboid, by its tonic contractility, fixes the base of the scapula against the thorax. If it be destroyed, the base of the scapula is removed from the thorax, and becomes prominent under the skin, so that a cavity is formed between the base of the scapula and the spine.

The *serratus magnus* is chiefly an inspiratory muscle; it elevates the ribs from which it arises; and contributes besides to lift the humerus. The arm is lifted above the horizontal line by the joint action of the deltoid, the serratus magnus, and the middle fibres of the trapezius. The serratus magnus also tends to keep the external angle of the scapula in its normal position; the weight of the upper extremity tending continually to depress the external angle of the scapula. Both the trapezius and the serratus are opposed to this depression being effected. If the trapezius be atrophied, the external angle of the scapula is depressed, while at the same time its inferior angle is raised and approached to the spinous processes; if the serratus be also attacked by wasting palsy, the external angle is still more depressed; the inferior angle is raised to the level of the external angle, and it moves at a considerable distance from the thorax.

68. Generally the most striking result of electro-muscular contractions is, an *increase of heat and bulk*, in the parts acted upon. On this point Dr. Ziemssen, of Greifswald, has made a series of experiments on healthy as well as on paralysed muscles, and has found that the augmentation of heat is proportional to the force of the contraction, and the length of time it continues. These contractions excite a sensation of heat in the shortened muscles, and are accompanied by an increase of bulk, which may be ¼ of an inch in the fore-arm, if the extensor muscles of the fore-arm are galvanised; and from ½ an inch to an inch in the thigh, if the rectus is galvanised. By means of the thermometer, and also by the hand, we are able to distinguish the heat communicated from the galvanised muscles to the skin which covers them, from the normal temperature of the surrounding parts. If the skin and the thermometer be covered by flannel, or any other substance which is a bad conductor of heat, the temperature rises more rapidly, and to a higher degree, than if they are uncovered. In both cases the heat produced is the same, and the apparent difference in the latter instance is merely due to the exclusion of air from the galvanised part, by

which means the heat generated is longer preserved.

The decrease of temperature, after the electric excitation has ceased, is slow and regular; but it is more rapid when the skin is exposed to the atmosphere than when it is covered.

The difference in the heat of the skin before and after the electric excitation of the muscles is in many cases 5° to 6° F.

I have made a number of experiments regarding the heat developed by electro-muscular contractions, especially on paralytic patients, which have led to the following conclusions:—

1. *The heat observed after Faradisation of the muscles is in no way due to the action of the current upon the skin.* This we may theoretically infer from the fact that, although the electrodes are in direct contact with the skin, the electric current, if applied by well-moistened electrodes, does not act on the skin at all, but traverses it, and penetrates to the muscles as the best conducting substance. This proposition is also affirmed by pathological experience. Some time ago I galvanised a patient suffering from lead-palsy; in this case the contractility of the extensor muscles of the *right* fore-arm was quite

abolished, while a certain contractility still remained in the extensor muscles of the *left* fore-arm. On applying induction currents for five minutes to the extensors of the left fore-arm, the temperature was increased from 89° F. to 91° 5′ F., while the same operation made on the extensors of the right fore-arm did not produce any increase of heat, but, on the contrary, the heat, which had been 87° 5′ in the right fore-arm before the application of electricity, was only 86° F. afterwards; this diminution of temperature being due to the contact of the skin of the fore-arm with the atmosphere.

2. *The increase of heat observed after Faradisation of the muscles, is not due to a greater afflux of blood to the arteries and veins,* for these are not expanded, but constricted by direct Faradisation, and consequently contain less blood after having been acted upon by induction-currents, than they do in their normal physiological condition.

3. *But the increase of heat observed after Faradisation of the muscles, is due to an augmentation of those chemical changes which are continually going on in the tissue of a muscle, and which constitute its nutrition.* The solid

structure of a muscle is permeated by a fluid, the composition of which is variable; muscular fluid taken from a muscle which has been at rest presents a neutral reaction, but when induction currents have been applied to a muscle, the fluid presents an acid re-action, in consequence of an augmented absorption of oxygen, and the formation of carbonic acid. If we measure the quantity of oxygen absorbed, and carbonic acid exhaled, by the muscular substance of frogs' thighs which have been skinned and suspended in vessels filled with air or oxygen, we find that if some of the muscles are galvanised, and the others not—the quantity of the gases absorbed and exhaled by the galvanised muscles is more than double that absorbed and exhaled during the same time by the quiescent muscles. The same differences occur in the living muscles of man; and, by the augmentation of chemical changes, the heat is increased, more blood is attracted to the capillary vessels of the muscular substance, whereby the bulk of the muscles is increased; and the very fact that there is more blood attracted to the tissue, produces again an increase in the nutrition of the parts.

4. *With regard to the direction of the current*, as in-

fluencing the increase of heat, I have generally remarked a slight difference in favour of the *direct* current—moving from the centre to the periphery—in healthy muscles; and an equally slight difference in favour of the *inverse* current—moving from the periphery to the centre—in paralysed muscles. I need not mention that in such comparative experiments the current applied was always of the same intensity, equally rapidly interrupted, and directed to the same muscles for the same length of time.

5. *As to the greater or less rapidity of the intermittences used,* I have invariably observed that the heat was increased more rapidly and to a higher degree, if a rapidly interrupted current was employed, than if the intermittences were slow.

69. I now proceed to consider the question, *how it is that galvanism acts beneficially in paralytic diseases;* a question which, up to the present time, has not been satisfactorily answered. It is obvious, that we can only arrive at a satisfactory solution of it, if we draw our conclusions from the established principles of electro-physiology, coupled with therapeutical experience.

First proposition.

The galvanic stimulus is capable of disturbing the molecular equilibrium of the motor nerves and muscles, so as to produce the state in which they are physiologically active. This disturbance, if judiciously produced, does not cause any injury, but tends to re-establish or to ameliorate the lost or impaired vitality of the motor nerves and muscles.

As the first part of this proposition flows directly from what has been described above, I need only say a few words on the latter part of it, which is an induction from my therapeutical experience.

There are two sorts of paralytic diseases which are often beneficially affected by the application of electricity, and in which by this proposition only we are able to explain the success of the treatment. I allude, in the first place, to cases in which the excitability of the paralysed muscles to the galvanic stimulus is completely *preserved*; and, in the second place, to cases in which the excitability of the paralysed muscles is totally *abolished*. Now if, as has often been contended, galvanism acted beneficially only by producing contraction, and thus improving the nutrition, of the paralysed muscles, cases like those just mentioned could not possibly be ameliorated or cured by electricity; since, in the former class of cases, the nutrition of the muscles is perfect, as they respond freely to a gentle current; and in the latter, no contraction of the muscles is produced. I have seen cases of cerebral and hysterical paralysis, in which the paralysed muscles had quite preserved their contractile power, considerably and rapidly ameliorated by Faradisation. I have also, by the same means, cured cases of rheumatic and of spontaneous paralysis, in which the nutrition of the muscles was not in the least impaired. It is highly probable that, in such cases, the paralysis depends upon a diminution or perversion of the current proper of the nerves and muscles, and that the current proper is restored to its normal condition by the application of electricity.

On the other hand, cases of lead-palsy and of traumatic paralysis are cured by electricity, although, in the commencement of the treatment, even a current of very high tension does not cause any movements whatever in the paralysed muscles. In such cases, the beneficial effect cannot be explained by the electric current producing contraction of the paralysed muscles; for no contractions are produced; nor by the current causing an increased supply of arterial blood to the limbs; for no increase is observable, either in the temperature or in the bulk of the muscles; but only by the supposition that the current restores that mobility to the molecules of the nerves and muscles which is necessary to enable them to be physiologically active.

Second Proposition.

The galvanic stimulus allows the necessary alternate contraction and expansion of the muscles, without which their nutrition is generally soon seriously impaired.

This fact having never been called in question, I merely adduce the evidence of the observations of Dr. John Reid, which are related in my "Treatise on Medical Electricity."

Third Proposition.

The galvanic stimulus, by producing contractions of the muscles, and thus augmenting the chemical changes in, that is, the oxidation of, the muscular tissue, causes a more abundant supply of arterial blood to it, which is evidenced by an increase of heat and bulk in those parts which have been galvanised, and which in its turn augments the nutrition of the muscle.

To sum up, galvanism acts in paralysis by restoring the lost mobility to the molecules of the nerves and muscles, and by causing contraction of, and a more considerable supply of arterial blood to, the paralysed muscles.

It now remains to determine the form of electricity which should be applied in paralytic diseases, the direction in which the current should be passed, the intensity of the current, and the length of time its action should be kept up.

As to the *form of electricity to be used in paralysis*, we must not in accordance with the electro-physiological law first established by Du Bois-Reymond, viz. that the motor nerves are not excited by the absolute amount of the density of the current, but merely by the variations which occur in the density of the current from one instant to the other; and that the amount of excitation caused is proportionate to the rapidity with which these changes take place. Hence it results that the continuous current should, as a rule, not be used in the treatment of paralysis, but induction currents, which consist of great and sudden variations, and are thereby capable of exciting the vitality of the motor nerves to the highest degree.

A singular objection has been raised by Dr. Golding Bird * against the current induced by voltaic electricity being an antiparalytic remedy. Dr. Bird thinks it necessary that the current should be sent through the paralysed muscles in the same direction in which the current proper of the muscles travels in the limbs. Now, he asserts that currents induced by voltaic electricity should not be employed for paralysis, as they are alternately guided in contrary directions. It is easy to refute this objection. In the first place, it is by no means proved that it is really necessary to send the current through the limbs in that particular direction; and in the second place, the physiological effect of the current induced on *making* the circuit is so extremely feeble that it must be disregarded altogether in therapeutical applications; it is only the current induced on *breaking* the circuit which exercises a remarkable physiological and therapeutical effect, and this current moves in a direction equal to that of the current of the battery.

Dr. Remak of Berlin, has recently published an account of the therapeutical action of the continuous current, which, according to him, is the

* Lectures on Electricity and Galvanism, &c. London, 1849.

true antiparalytic remedy, and especially useful in brain disease and atrophy of the spinal cord; in which complaints the most wonderful cures are said to have been obtained by him in an incredibly short time. During a visit to France, Dr. Remak made some therapeutical experiments with the continuous current before colleagues in Paris, on the results of which Dr. Déchambre has given the following report in the Gazette Hebdomadaire:

"From four patients galvanised under our eyes, two were in such a condition that we should have been much surprised to see any improvement produced in a few moments. The first was a case of general wasting palsy, especially marked in the upper extremities. The muscles of the shoulder were electrified, but the movement of elevation of the arm has thereby not become easier. The second had a treble lateral curvature of the spine, in consequence of a deviation of the pelvis to the left side, resulting from sciatica. It was tried to redress the middle and inferior curvatures by the excitation of the muscles in the convexity; but without any appreciable result. The two other cases seemed to offer more chances; for in the one there was an incomplete paralysis of the deltoid, in a very young man, in consequence of a contusion; in the other paralysis of the extensors of the hand, ascribed to a cause of the same kind; but here also no effect was produced."

These results do, of course, not show that the continuous current has no antiparalytic effects; they only show that Dr. Remak has exaggerated its beneficial action. The instances in which the continuous current may be expected to produce benefit, will be mentioned hereafter.

No rules are at present fixed as to the *direction* in which the induced current should be sent through the paralysed limbs. We know that the current in the arm of man travels from the shoulder towards the hand; hence it has been concluded that it would be best to send the induced current through the nerves in the same direction; that is to say, to use the *direct* current. On the contrary, Matteucci has recommended that in paralysis of motion the current administered should be *inverse;* as he supposes that the nerves of the affected limb might be in a condition similar to that which is caused by the prolonged passage of a direct continuous current through a limb; and as we may by administering an *inverse* current to the nerve of a frog's leg restore to the nerve the excitability which it has been deprived of by the passage of the *direct* current, so Matteucci supposed the current would more readily relieve the paralysis of motion in man, if it were sent through the motor nerves, which act centrifugally, in the inverse or centripetal direction; while paralysis of sensation would require the centrifugal or direct current, since the sentient nerves act centripetally. However ingenious this theory may be, there are no proofs whatever of its being correct; and its practical value seems to be very doubtful. Besides, it applies strictly to the continuous current only, and not to the induced current. A more palpable reason for employing the inverse current in the treatment of paralysis is, that in many cases of paralysis the inverse current excites stronger contractions in the muscles than the direct; hence it appears justifiable to use the inverse current with preference in such cases. It is, however, important to change now and then the direction of the current, as by the continued passage of a current always guided in the same direction, the motor nerves and muscles may be fatigued.

As to the *intensity* of the current to be employed, it is necessary exactly to measure the dose which may be convenient for each case; therefore we should always begin with a very gentle current and gradually increase its intensity, so as to produce, if possible, decided contractions of the paralysed muscles. Severe shocks, especially in the commencement of the treatment, should be carefully avoided, as by such the weakened excitability of the motor nerves may be still further reduced.

No general directions can be given as to the *duration* of each operation, which must be left to the judgment of the Physician. Some cases require long applications, others do better if the operations be not of too long duration. Generally speaking, however, the electric current should not be administered for more than a quarter of an hour each time.

The *number* of operations required to cure paralytic diseases is also very variable. Cases of hysterical paralysis not unfrequently require only a few applications of electricity. Thus I have cured a case of hysterical aphonia and two cases of amenorrhœa by only one operation each; other cases require a longer treatment, and in cases of wasting palsy or Cruveilhier's atrophy, a very large number of operations must be performed in order to arrest the disease, and to ameliorate the patient's condition.

Cerebral Paralysis.

Some cases of this kind are likely to be benefited by electricity, while others are not; and this depends entirely upon the pathological process which is going on within the cranium.

There are three principal classes of cases; in the first the muscles of the paralysed limb are relaxed, the limbs loose and flaccid, and if the forearm is flexed upon the arm, or the leg upon the thigh, there is no resistance to that movement. The paralysed muscles present a striking contrast to the firmness and plumpness of those of the sound side, and they are more or less wasted according to the length of time which has elapsed since the paralytic seizure. In such cases, there is generally very little response to the galvanic stimulus, and the heat and general nutrition of the limbs is much below par. Some of these cases recover of themselves, in others a partial recovery only takes place after a certain time. If four to six months or more have elapsed since the seizure, and the recovery is imperfect, it is justifiable to employ electricity in cases of this kind. It is, however, important that the electric current should be localised in those muscles which remain paralysed and really require the stimulus. Therefore the excitors—moistened sponges lodged in metallic cylinders—are to be held as close as possible to each other on the skin, in order to limit the current of the muscles covered by it. When the excitors are held removed from each other, so that the electric current passes through the whole length of the limbs,—for instance, when one excitor is held in the right, and the other one in the left hand; or if the feet of a patient be placed in two separate vessels filled with salt water and connected with the poles of a battery, —painful and irregular commotions are caused in the paralysed and the healthy muscles, which are indiscriminately affected. Consequently, this method of operation can scarcely ever be beneficial to the patient. As to the intermittences of the induced current, they should be rather slow, whereby any irritation of the brain is avoided. I shall now relate a case, in which only a few muscles remained paralysed after the paralytic seizure, and in which a considerable amelioration was effected by the faradic treatment.

Case 11. *Paralysis from Apoplexy.*

Jane S., a cook, aged 35, was under the care of

Dr. Alderson, in St. Mary's Hospital, in July, 1857. She had had an apoplectic attack fifteen months before, in which she lost her consciousness, and the use of the left arm and leg. The latter soon regained some power; but the deltoid muscle, the extensor of the forefinger and all the muscles of the thumb were still paralysed when I first saw her; they were quite flaccid, and their bulk had considerably diminished. She was not able to wash, cook, or do needle-work. When I directed an extra-current of five centimètres power to the paralysed muscles, they showed very little excitability. After five operations, the deltoid muscle was so much improved, that the patient could again raise the arm to a right angle with the body; but the muscles of the forefinger and the thumb only got better after a longer treatment. I attended the patient for about a month, after which she left the hospital, being again able to return to her business.

In another class of cases, the muscles, which are paralysed in consequence of brain disease, exhibit a certain amount of rigidity, which is especially remarkable in the biceps of the arm and the hamstring muscles of the thigh; and which varies from an increased plumpness up to a contraction almost tetanic. Dr. Todd has termed this the state of *early rigidity*, as it exists either from the moment of the attack, or soon after it has taken place. In such cases the circulation in the limb is vigorous, the heat not below par, and the paralysed muscles generally more excitable to the galvanic stimulus than those of the healthy limb. In cases of this kind other remedies have to be employed before the therapeutical application of electricity can be of avail.

Finally, the muscles may present the state of *late rigidity*. Muscles which have been flaccid and wasted for a certain time, gradually acquire more tension and become shortened. The tendency to assume this rigid state is more marked in the arm than in the leg, and more in the flexor muscles than in the extensors. It is generally caused by the gradual shrinking of the cyst, which operates as an irritant foreign body on the brain. In most of these cases, the electric treatment should not be resorted to; but in some cases of long standing, an electric excitation of those muscles which are the antagonists of the rigid muscles, may serve to restore the disturbed equilibrium between the sets of muscles. The following case may serve to illustrate this:

Case 12. *Paralysis from Apoplexy.*

In December, 1858, a man of the name of Marsh was in King's College Hospital, under the care of Dr. Todd. Four years ago he had had an apoplectic attack with consequent paralysis of the right side. The paralysed muscles had then soon assumed a state of rigidity, which has not undergone any considerable change since that time. At present the patient can with some difficulty walk, but the right arm is perfectly useless, as there exists a rigidity of a number of muscles; viz., of the coraco-brachial muscle, whereby the arm is adducted to the side; of the biceps, so that the fore-arm is bent upon the arm; if forcible extension of the fore-arm is attempted, the biceps offers a certain resistance to it, but no pain is experienced during the forcible extension. Stiffness is also marked in the triceps, although much less than in the biceps; it becomes evident if a complete flexion of the fore-arm upon the arm is attempted so as to place the fingers on the acromion of the same side. The flexor muscles of the wrist and of the fingers are in a state of complete rigidity; the hand is strongly bent upon the fore-arm, and the fingers are firmly pressed against the palm of the hand, so that the patient is obliged to cut his nails very short, in order to prevent irritation of the skin by the growth of the nails. The tendons project like tight strings beneath the skin. The patient affirms, however, that he experiences no pain if a forcible extension of the wrist and of the fingers is attempted. There is not much wasting in the muscles, but the excitability to the galvanic stimulus is very very trifling in the extensor muscles of the fore-arm, while the flexors of the fore-arm contract very readily under the influence of a gentle current. The stiffness of the muscles of the lower extremity is much less considerable than of those of the arm; it is, however, distinct in the ham-string muscles and in the flexors of the toes; and in walking the patient drags the paralysed leg.

In consultation with Dr. Todd, I gave the opinion that in this case the cyst had shrunk to a very small volume, and that the disturbance in the equilibrium between the different sets of muscles of the upper extremity was no longer exclusively due to the lesion of the brain, which was undoubtedly the primitive cause of it, but mostly to the long continued predominance of the contracted flexors over the paralysed extensors of the fore-arm; and I thought that by administering a suitable stimulus to the relaxed extensors the equilibrium between the two sets of muscles might be restored. This view was confirmed by the result of the treatment; for after I had faradised the extensor muscles of the fore-arm for some time, the tendons of the flexors, which had before projected like tight strings beneath the skin, became soft and flexible; and the patient was able to open his hand and stretch his fingers; but having been some time afterwards exposed to a violent cold draught, the flexors again assumed a certain degree of rigidity. Unfortunately there was at that time no battery in King's College Hospital furnishing a continuous current of electricity, which I should have wished to apply to the rigid flexors, or the patient's condition might have been much more ameliorated. By further Faradisation he again improved, but he left the hospital before a permanent relief was afforded.

The following case may show how much benefit may result from a combined application of the continuous and the induced current in paralysis with late rigidity of the muscles:—

Case 13. *Paralysis from Apoplexy.*

A. B., aged 63, had had an apoplectic attack in

September, 1859, accompanied with loss of consciousness and entire cessation of voluntary movements. Some months afterwards the flexor muscles, which had at first been flaccid, became rigid, while the extensors wasted away rapidly. The affection was much more considerable in the arm than in the leg. The patient consulted me in March, 1863, when, from the long standing of the affection, the opinion was entertained that a cure was not to be thought of. The treatment consisted in Faradisation of the muscles animated by the radial nerve, and in Galvanisation (by from 18 to 20 cells) of the median, ulnar, and sciatic nerves. Under the influence of this treatment, the rigidity of the flexor muscles gradually subsided, and the extensors simultaneously gained very much in bulk and power. After a month the patient, who, when he came to me, could not take off his hat, or pick up a pencil, and walked with great difficulty, was able to dress and feed himself, write a perfectly legible hand, and could walk two or three miles at a time without fatigue.

Spinal Paralysis.

In this form of paralysis both Galvanisation and Faradisation are extremely useful, although I doubt whether they ever effect a radical cure. Whether the treatment is likely to be successful or not, depends chiefly upon the cause and duration of the disease, and upon the age and constitution of the patient. If the paralysis is caused by tumours pressing on the spinal cord, or if the vertebral column is diseased, or if the marrow is destroyed by inflammation and softening, the electric current may relieve certain symptoms of the affection, but cannot have any permanent beneficial effects. On the contrary, if the paralysis is caused by over-exertion and consequent exhaustion of nervous power, by rheumatism, by embolism of the vertebral artery and its branches, or where the affection occurs in children during teething, the greatest benefit may result from a judicious use of Faradisation and Galvanisation. *Cæteris paribus*, young patients and recent cases are more likely to get well than the reverse.

Case 14. *Paraplegia due to disease of the spinal cord in the dorsal region.*

T. B., aged 35, a surveyor, had, with the exception of gonorrhœa, never been ill until six months ago, when he was unusually over-taxed with work, and was constantly exposed to the influence of damp and cold. So gradual was the loss of power that came over him, that he did not notice it himself first, but was told by his friends that his gait was tottering. Soon afterwards, however, he felt so weak that he could not walk without the aid of a stick. He mentioned that his feet used to perspire a good deal before he was affected with this disease, but had not done so after he had begun to suffer from it.

In the region of the tenth dorsal vertebra, the back was very painful to pressure, and hot sponges applied there, produced a peculiarly unpleasant sensation, different from that which was felt on the other parts of the back. The patient had at first perceived sensations as of pins and needles in the lower extremities; these sensations were, after a time, succeeded by a feeling of considerable numbness, so that he did not feel the ground when walking. As soon as he shut his eyes, or when in the dark, he began to stagger. Going downstairs was especially difficult for him. The skin was dry, cold, and flaccid. I examined it by the aid of the æsthesiometer, and found a great diminution of sensibility all over the lower part of the back, the epigastrium, and the lower extremities; but there was no complete anæsthesia.

The muscles of the abdomen and of the lower extremities were somewhat wasted, and sluggish in their response to the galvanic stimulus. The patient suffered from costiveness and a feeling of pressure and tightness in the epigastrium, and was obliged to use great exertions for relieving the bladder. The urine was apt to turn alkaline in a short time, but otherwise healthy. The patient had sometimes involuntary emissions of fæces and urine. He had taken much medicine, especially strychnia, bichloride of mercury, and iodide of potassium, but without any benefit.

The diagnosis was: chronic myelitis in the dorsal region, due to over-exertion and exposure; the treatment to consist of Galvanisation of the back and the feet, and Faradisation of the muscles of the abdomen and of the lower extremities. No medicine was given. The result was as follows:—The feet, to which a current of thirty cells of Bunsen's battery was administered, became warm and glowing after a short time, and the pain in the back, for which a current of twelve cells was used, was very much diminished. After a fortnight's treatment the patient felt a good deal better. He had more control over his lower extremities, was better able to hold and let his urine, and sensation was more distinct everywhere. He remained under my care for nearly six weeks, gradually getting stronger, and being again able to walk a short distance without the aid of a stick. The feet now perspired just as much as they had ever done before, and from the time this secretion was re-established, the pain in the back was so much relieved that the patient no longer complained of it. In this case, I do not think it impossible that by a longer treatment a cure might have been effected, as the mischief in the spinal cord had evidently not proceeded to destruction of the nervous matter.

Local palsies of motor nerves and voluntary muscles.

Of all the cerebral nerves the portio dura is the one most frequently affected with local paralysis. The three nerves which animate the muscles of the eye are also liable to this disease; but if there are symptoms of the eighth nerve being paralysed, there is probably disease in that part of the brain where this complex nerve takes its origin.

1. *Palsies of the muscles of the eye.*

If the *third nerve*, or motor oculi, is paralysed,

the eyelid cannot be raised in consequence of loss of power in the levator palpebræ superioris muscle; this dropping of the upper eyelid (ptosis) is the most constant symptom of paralysis of the third nerve. Other signs of this affection are protrusion of the eyeball, and dilatation of the pupil, which cannot be turned inwards, while the outward movement is not impaired, since the rectus externus is animated by the sixth nerve. The upward and downward motion of the eyeball is limited or quite impossible; besides, there is double vision, and the accommodation of the eye for the vision of objects near the patient is impossible.

Local palsy of the *fourth nerve* is of very rare occurrence, and difficult to be recognised. Dr. A. von Graefe, of Berlin, has observed that in this affection the pupil is turned a little upwards and inwards; when looking upwards, vision is not disturbed, but in looking at an object placed horizontally before the eye, the patient is troubled by double vision; and to avoid this, the head is generally turned towards the opposite side.

If the *sixth nerve* is paralysed, the patient squints inwards, and is troubled by double vision in certain directions; sometimes the inward deviation of the eye is so strong that the whole cornea may be concealed at the inner angle of the orbit. This palsy generally occurs simultaneously with a similar affection of the third nerve; and then the globe can neither be moved upwards, nor outwards, nor downwards.

These palsies may be caused by affections of the brain; but they have seldom been observed as the only symptoms of such diseases. They are more frequently caused by rheumatic or syphilitic exudations, and over-exertion, or want of exertion, of the muscles; tumours may also compress the substance of the muscles or nerves. Certain cases are incurable, others get well after they have existed for some time without any treatment whatever. The treatment generally adopted consists of, 1st, gymnastic exercise of the affected muscles, which is, of course, only possible, if the paralysis is incomplete; and, 2ndly, excitation of the skin in the neighbourhood of the eye. In cases which are traceable to over-exertion, or want of exertion, or an effusion which is not of a syphilitic character, Faradisation deserves a trial. Three different methods have been adopted in the application of electricity to the paralysed muscles of the eye, viz., by placing one electrode in the hand of the patient, and touching the skin in the neighbourhood of the eye with the other electrode; by faradising the branches of the trigeminal and facial nerves, in order to excite the nerves and muscles of the eye by reflex action; and finally, by electro-puncture, viz., introduction of needles connected with the poles of a battery into the tissue of the paralysed muscles. The best way is, however, to place one electrode connected with the negative pole into the hand of the patient, and to apply a small moistened sponge connected with the positive pole to the skin of the closed eye, as close as possible to the paralysed muscle. For exciting the rectus internus the positive electrode should be held to the inner angle of the eye; and for localising the electric current in the obliquus superior, the positive electrode is to be placed beneath the trochlea. In this way patients suffering from paralysis of the several muscles of the eye have been successfully treated by Dr. Meyer, of Berlin, Mr. Soelberg Wells, and myself.

2. *Paralysis of the facial nerve.*

There are two different kinds of facial palsy; one arising from exposure to a draught of cold air, and generally caused by a rheumatic effusion in the cellular tissue, between the facial muscles and the exterior branches of the portio dura; the other arising from injury to the intracranial portion of the facial nerve. In the former class of cases the muscular and nervous fibres are compressed, and their function cohibited by the effusion; in such cases there is no destruction or inflammation of the nerve, and the paralysis disappears in proportion as the effusion is absorbed. Therefore it may happen that some of the facial muscles soon regain their normal power, while others remain paralysed; but if any injury has happened to the trunk of the portio dura within the cranium, the affection is almost invariably the same in all the physiognomical muscles. The absorption of the rheumatic effusion is often spontaneous, and many cases of facial palsy get well without any treatment whatever. In some cases amelioration is induced by blistering and the application of an ointment of iodide of potassium, etc. In other cases these means prove insufficient to induce absorption of the effusion, which in time may become hard and callous. In all cases of this kind the faradic stimulus is the best means of restoring the muscles to their normal state, by causing them to contract individually, and inducing a more or less rapid absorption of the effusion. Generally the excitability of the muscles to the faradic stimulus is impaired, and the tone and the voluntary movements of the muscles return in proportion as the excitability of the muscles is restored.

In facial palsy, the physiognomical expressions of surprise, terror, hilarity, threat, sadness, reflection, malice, disgust, and rage, vanish on the paralysed side, and are exaggerated on the sound side; the patient is not able to frown, laugh, or whistle; besides which certain changes in the features, which depend upon the disturbance of the equilibrium between the paralysed and non-paralysed muscles, take place. If both sides of the face are paralysed, the features appear as if covered by a mask, and the eyeballs only are capable of motion.

If the frontal portion of the *occipito-frontalis* muscle and the *corrugator supercilii* are paralysed, the patient is not able to move the scalp nor to frown. Where the forehead is wrinkled, as is the case in old people, the transverse wrinkles disappear by paralysis of the frontal muscle, and the perpendicular wrinkles between the eyebrows vanish by loss of power in the corrugator.

In certain cases the eyebrow is seen to drop and hang above the orbit; which gives the face a doleful, and in some instances a truly terrible, expression.

If the *orbicularis palpebrarum* is paralysed the eye cannot be shut; it is consequently always exposed to the air, even during sleep, whereby in many cases a state of irritation in the conjunctiva is caused. Tears flow freely, and to such an extent that the skin of the cheek may be excoriated by them. The conjunctiva is often injected, but such changes in the nutrition of the cornea and of the conjunctiva as are observed in anæsthesia of the fifth pair, never take place. The eye generally appears staring and protruded, the eyelids are further apart than is natural, and a large portion of the sclerotic is exposed to view; this is especially caused by the dropping of the lower eyelid. If the patient is told to shut the eye, either no motion is perceptible, or the eyeball is carried upwards and inwards beneath the upper eyelid, so that the cornea is partially or totally concealed; the latter movement being executed by the rectus internus, rectus superior, and obliquus inferior muscles, which are not animated by the portio dura, but by the third pair. The eyelids are apart, because the levator palpebræ superioris muscle, which is the antagonist of the orbicularis, retains its power, it being likewise animated by the third pair. Paralysis of the orbicularis does not occur in facial hemiplegia of central origin, so that if the eye cannot be shut, we may be sure that the case is one of paralysis of the portio dura, and not of cerebral paralysis.

In facial palsy the nostril is devoid of voluntary movements, in consequence of the paralysis of the *levator alæ nasi*, and *pyramidalis nasi*. Thus dilatation of the corresponding nostril becomes impossible, and it is kept open only by the rigidity of the cartilages of the nose. The respiratory movements, as far as they regard the motion of the nostril, are opposite in paralysis of the portio dura to that which they are in the normal state; for while in the normal state the nostrils are dilated during inspiration, and constricted during expiration, they become in facial palsy constricted during inspiration by the air rushing into the lungs, and dilated during expiration by the air being driven out from the lungs.

Paralysis of the muscles of the ear, which are animated by the facial nerve, does not betray itself by any symptoms, since the human ear is kept in its ordinary position by the rigidity of its cartilages. On the contrary, in animals the ears of which are soft and long, as is the case in the rabbit and the ass, the ears droop after section of the facial nerves.

By paralysis of the *zygomatici* muscles, and the *levator anguli oris*, the angle of the mouth appears depressed and pendant, and is drawn towards the opposite side; the angle of the mouth of the sound side, on the contrary, appears higher, and is drawn towards the ear.

Paralysis of the *buccinator* muscle causes the cheek to appear very flaccid and hang loosely, whereby the face appears old. During inspiration the cheek becomes depressed, while during expiration it cannot resist the pressure of the air, and therefore becomes distended and swelled; thus a movement is produced the same as that made in smoking a pipe. Mastication is generally not much impaired, since the temporal and the masseter muscles are not animated by the portio dura, but by the trigeminal nerve; but eating, nevertheless, becomes troublesome, as, in consequence of the paralysis of the buccinator, the food, after having been chewed, becomes accumulated between the jaw and the cheek, which latter is swelled by it; and not unfrequently the patient is obliged to use his hand for bringing the food under the teeth; and, on drinking, the fluid runs out at the corner of the mouth. The speech is likewise rendered somewhat difficult by the looseness of the cheek.

If the *orbicularis oris* is paralysed, the patient is unable to purse up his mouth and to whistle, the lips are drawn to the opposite side and appear longer, the sulcus naso-labialis is more prominent, and an involuntary flow of saliva is observed. Besides, the pronunciation of the labials is rendered very difficult.

Such are the symptoms if the superficial branches of the facial nerve are paralysed; but if the facial nerve is injured in its intra-cranial portion, other symptoms are generally connected with those related before; viz. loss of taste with a feeling of numbness in the tongue, caused by paralysis of the *chorda tympani;* difficulty of deglutition, by paralysis of those branches of the facial nerve which animate the muscles *digastricus* and *stylo-hyoides;* deviation of the uvula; and the hearing is affected. In some cases it has been noticed that the patient was able to move the tongue, but not to such an extent as to cover the upper lip by it. Deep-seated palsies of the portio dura are produced by inflammation of the sheath of the facial nerve, by fracture, caries or necrosis of the petrous portion of the temporal bone, and are often associated with otitis; but they are scarcely ever a symptom of primary brain disease. The brain, however, may afterwards become affected, if the disease extends from the temporal bone to the meninges and the medullary substance. In all cases which result from injury to the trunk of the portio dura, benefit can only be expected from an electric treatment, when the original lesion has nearly or totally subsided; but if the continuity of the fibres of the facial nerve has been quite destroyed, the palsy is incurable. In some cases it happens that, after the paralysis has existed for a certain time, a permanent contraction of the paralysed muscles takes place; it is evident that nothing can be expected from electricity in such instances. But when the nerve has regained its normal condition, facial palsy is generally cured by a judicious faradic treatment, even if the case be of very long standing. Professor Oré has related a case of facial palsy of eight and a half years' duration, which was cured by electricity, and Dr. Russell Reynolds mentions a case of fourteen years' standing which was notably improved by electricity. It is, however, necessary to state that in advanced age the probability of the cure is less. From many cases of this kind which have come under my observation, I select the following:

Case 15. *Paralysis of the Face.*

Mr. F., a barrister, aged 35, was, in consequence of having been exposed to a draught of cold air at a railway station, affected with paralysis of the left facial nerve. The physiognomical expression had entirely vanished from that side of the face. The patient was not able to laugh, to frown, to whistle, or to shut his eye, which latter appeared staring and protruded. The angle of the mouth was depressed, and drawn towards the opposite side; that of the sound side being higher and drawn towards the ear. The cheek was flaccid and loose; and eating and speaking was troublesome. The patient was sent to me by the late Dr. Todd, whom he had consulted six months after the commencement of the affection. I directed the Faradic stimulus to all the paralysed muscles individually, with the effect that the patient regained his normal physiognomical expression, after a fortnight's treatment.

Before concluding these observations, I will

mention an interesting case of the same affection, which seems to show that, in certain cases, a lightning stroke may have curative powers.

Lightning may kill at a blow, or induce blindness, deafness, and other diseases of a paralytic as well as a spasmodic character, which, however alarming they may appear at first, generally subside in a few days, and scarcely ever last longer than some months; but it undoubtedly has sometimes also the beneficial effect of an electric current of moderate intensity, and may cause the cure of rheumatic, paralytic, and spasmodic conditions. No doubt most of the numerous cases described as cures by lightning are either fabulous or greatly exaggerated, but the very existence of so many reports seem to infer some small degree of truth.

The case I have just referred to is that of Samuel Leffers, of Carteret County, North Carolina, U.S., which is generally quoted as an instance of amaurosis or general paralysis cured by lightning, and which occurred in 1806. In the United States, the most marvellous particulars were circulated of the case, and Professor Olmsted, who has recorded it,* states that henceforth it was

* American Journal of Arts and Sciences, vol. iii. p. 100, 1821.

generally believed, that under certain circumstances lightning would suddenly change decrepit old age into blooming youth. Thus it was related of Mr. Leffers, a very old man, who had been so much paralysed that he was no longer able to walk or even stand, and whose features were frightfully distorted, that he had through a lightning shock suddenly regained the full force of his youth and an exquisitely beautiful complexion and soft skin, and that he had retained this complete youth up to his ninetieth year. The *facts* of the case are, however, as follows:—Samuel Leffers was affected by what is now generally known as paralysis of the portio dura, and which in most cases is only a troublesome and annoying, but by no means dangerous, affection. At the time, however, when this occurred, medical diagnosis had not advanced so far as it is at present, and this affection was not distinguished from paralysis of the face due to hemiplegia, and was therefore considered as a certain sign of the immediate break-up of the patient's constitution. That Samuel Leffers' complaint was in fact nothing more than paralysis of certain branches of the facial nerve is evident from the description of his symptoms, which were as follows:—On awakening one morning he felt an unpleasant numbness in the left side of the face; he could not shut the left eye, and his speech was impaired. These symptoms "caused him to believe that he had been affected by a paralytic stroke." Some time afterwards the disease improved in the other parts of the face, and centred in the eye, which he could not shut day or night; it was consequently exposed to obnoxious influences and the sight became much impaired; that is to say, the buccinator and other muscles recovered their tone, while the orbicularis palpebrarum still remained paralysed. He was in this state, when, one day, while walking in the hall of his house during a storm, he was struck by lightning. He fell down, and remained unconscious from fifteen to twenty minutes, when he recovered so far as to be able to distinguish objects around him, and to be conscious of his position. During the night he fully regained the use of his senses and limbs, and felt so well the following morning, that he resolved to write an account of what had happened to him, to a friend. He then supposed that, as he had not been able to see well for some time, his note must necessarily be a short one; but he was astonished to find that he could write a long letter without experiencing any inconvenience, the last remains of the paralysis having entirely disappeared; nor did it again return. He had thus been effectually cured from his previous complaint; but his hearing had, at the same time, become weak, and he always afterwards complained of a certain degree of deafness. From this description, it is quite evident that the orbicularis palpebrarum muscle, which had been paralysed, was beneficially affected by the stroke; but the case was neither one of amaurosis, nor one of general paralysis cured by lightning.

Difficulty of Deglutition.

Paralytic affections of the tongue and the pharynx ought to excite our suspicion, as they are generally indicative of mischief in the brain. But even in such instances improvement may result from a judicious use of electricity, as will be seen by the following :—

Case 16. *Paralysis from Brain Disease; hoarseness and difficulty of deglutition.*

Major ——, aged 42, consulted me in September, 1862, for loss of voice and difficulty of deglutition, brought on by an apoplectic attack, which he had had in 1859, and which affected the entire left side of the body. For several months after this he had been in such a condition that his life was despaired of. He gradually, however, got better, and partially recovered the use of his arm and leg, while the voice and deglutition did not improve. The latter symptom even became worse as time went on, there being constant regurgitation especially of fluids, which distressed the patient more than anything else. After a fortnight's Faradisation, the patient attending every day, the voice was so much improved that he could converse with ease, while the power of swallowing had not yet returned. I then applied a continuous current of ten cells to the pharyngeal and œsophageal nerves, with the effect that after the second operation a most remarkable improvement took place; and after a week the patient was able to swallow quite easily and without any regurgitation taking place. At the same time the arm and leg, which had been subjected to the influence of Faradisation, had, in a great measure, regained their power. The voice, however, still remained somewhat hoarse, and prolonged conversation was fatiguing.

Paralysis of the Vocal Cords.

The introduction of the laryngoscope into medical practice has facilitated the diagnosis of diseases of the larynx in the most wonderful manner; and consequently the treatment of these affections is now more easy, safe and successful than it could have been before. Where loss of voice is due to inflammation, ulceration, or morbid growths in the larynx, a special lo^al treatment by caustics, astringents, the *écraseur*, etc., has to be resorted to; but where the affection arises from mere loss of power in the vocal cords, Faradisation of the recurrent nerve, or of the vocal cords themselves, is the best treatment. Such loss of power is frequent in hysterical girls, but it also occurs after certain acute diseases, such as typhoid fever and diphtheria, in poisoning by arsenic, in anæmia, and as a consequence of over-exertion of the voice, or of a powerful impression upon the nervous centres, such as terror, fright, etc. In such cases the voice not unfrequently comes back after a time without any treatment whatever having been resorted to; but there are very numerous instances in which it does not return for years, and all treatment is unsuccessful, except the galvanic.

The first cure of loss of voice by galvanism was effected as far back as 1800, when a German physician, Dr. Grapengiesser, of Berlin, thought of trying the effect of the current of a single pair on the throat of a girl who had lost her voice for several years. He first vesicated each side of the larynx by blisters of the size of a shilling, and then applied the zinc pole to one of the excoriated spots, the silver pole to the other. The circuit was then kept up for a quarter of an hour, during which time the larynx heaved convulsively, and a great quantity of serous fluid flowed from the wounds. The sobbing continued after the metals had been removed, much mucus was expectorated, and two hours afterwards the voice was much more audible and clear. After this process had been repeated several times, the voice was perfectly restored. Six months afterwards, however, it was suddenly lost again in consequence of a cold, and it did not again return, although the process of Galvanisation was repeated. A similar case, in which the same therapeutical proceeding was adopted, has been recorded in the Dublin Quarterly Journal for February, 1847. In this instance, the improvement began on the evening of the day when galvanism was first applied, and continued until the fourth day, when the voice was again lost. The process was then repeated, and the apparatus left on all night, with the effect of permanently restoring the voice.

Professor Sédillot has published a case of complete dumbness and aphonia, which had existed for twelve years, in a woman thirty years of age. In this case the movements of the tongue were much impaired, the organ being retracted and directed upwards, and the patient not being able to bring the apex of the tongue in contact with the teeth. Professor Sédillot ordered the application of induction currents; one pole was placed alternately on different parts of the tongue, the other on the mastoid process, the posterior and superior part of the neck, and various points of the face. Some pain was experienced, and a severe head-ache followed this application. A week afterwards a second *séance* was held, after which the patient began to talk distinctly, though the voice had not as yet quite returned. A few more applications effected a complete cure.

Duchenne has published two cases of hysterical aphonia, one of six months', the other more than two years' standing; both cases were cured by the application of induction currents to the larynx.

Duchenne also adds that he has been unsuccessful in other cases, but he does not give the proportion of successes and failures.

I have had ample opportunity of trying the value of Faradisation in the treatment of this affection, as I have been fortunate enough to see thirty-nine cases of it. For most of them I am obliged to the Physicians of the Samaritan Free Hospital. All the patients were women, and most of them under thirty years of age; fifteen were married, and twenty-four single. In no case were there signs of inflammation, or of ulceration of the mucous membrane of the larynx, which would have accounted for the loss of voice; but the affection consisted merely in loss of nervous power in the vocal cords. Some patients stated a cold draught to have been the cause of the loss of the voice; others did not know how it was brought on, as, awaking in the morning, they found the voice gone.

The degree of the affection was different. The normal "timbre" of the voice was totally lost in all cases, but most of the patients were able to whisper by movements of the lips and tongue. Such whispering was quite distinct in some patients, but hardly intelligible in others, two of which were observed in King's College Hospital, under the care of Dr. Todd, another in the Samaritan Free Hospital, under the care of Dr, Savage. A sore feeling in the throat was complained of by all the patients; some of them also felt pain in the chest, and in the epigastrium. Twenty were irregular as to the time of entrance of the catamenia; but amenorrhœa was not present in any of them. In two cases aphonia was only one symptom of a deep hysterical disturbance of the whole nervous system, as these patients suffered besides from globus hystericus, violent head-ache, sleepiness, cramps, and weakness in the limbs; one of them afterwards passed into a cataleptic state.

To give Faradisation a fair trial, in most of these cases either indifferent drugs or no medicine was given. The current was, by means of moistened conductors, directed to the recurrent nerve, and where this did not prove successful, Faradisation of the skin was resorted to. This mode of application proved beneficial, as out of thirty-nine cases thirty were cured in a short time. Faradisation proved unsuccessful in nine cases, most of which were of long standing, and complicated with other symptoms of hysteria. In the majority of cases the voice, when it came back, was at once quite as strong as it had ever been before; while in some others an increase in the strength of the voice was discernible from the beginning to the end of the treatment. The following case was one of peculiar interest:—

Case 17. *Loss of Voice.*

A woman, aged 30, was sent to me by Dr. Rasch, in May, 1862, she having lost her voice two months before. An examination of her throat, by means of the laryngoscope, showed that the loss of voice was due to a paralytic condition of both vocal cords, which were perfectly motionless, and between which a considerable cleft was visible. After two operations, the patient could speak again, though still in a hoarse tone only. It was then discovered, by the aid of the laryngoscope, that the right vocal cord had, to a great extent recovered, and approached the middle line when the patient endeavoured to pronounce a prolonged "ah," but there was as yet no improvement in the left. This is an interesting physiological fact, showing that the normal state of one vocal cord is sufficient for the production of certain vocal sounds. By further treatment, the left vocal cord was also restored to its normal condition, and the voice entirely recovered.

Dr. Morell Mackenzie has lately invented an instrument for the direct application of electricity to the vocal cords, and which promises to be successful in cases where the external galvanic treatment is of no avail. This instrument, which is introduced while the laryngoscope is used, consists of a long electrode furnished with a spring, by means of which two metal rings may be connected with, or withdrawn from, each other, so that the operator, by pressing a handle, can make the current act, while by relaxing the pressure, the effect ceases at once. Care must be taken to employ a gentle current, as otherwise the stimulation of the pneumogastric nerve might prove dangerous.

Reflex Paralysis.

This form of paralysis, which is due to an irritation proceeding from a sensitive nerve, and thence transmitted to the spinal cord, is frequently cured as soon as the irritation is removed; in many cases, however, even after the cessation of the cause, the paralysis remains; and then Faradisation is the best means to bring about recovery. Again, in many cases, Faradisation or Galvanisation may remove the irritation, and thus exercise a curative action. These propositions will be best understood, if illustrated by a few cases.

Case 18. *Reflex paralysis of the hand, after amputation of a finger.*

Mrs. D., aged 42, pricked the forefinger of her left hand with a needle. This induced considerable pain, of which she did not at first take much notice; but as the finger soon became much inflamed, she applied for medical advice. Notwithstanding the treatment she underwent, the inflammation increased, gangrene ensued, and at last amputation of the finger became necessary. This operation was performed by Mr. Spencer Wells, on the 23rd of December, 1858. Three months elapsed before the stump was healed, as at first the pus was of a very bad character; and the secretion only improved after repeated cauterisation with nitrate of silver. When the citatrix had at last been formed, it appeared that the patient had entirely lost the use of her hand, and she was then sent to me by Mr. Spencer Wells. When I first saw her, the fingers were extended and quite stiff; flexion and lateral movements were impossible. The forearm could only with difficulty be bent, and every movement of it was painful. Numbness was felt in all the fingers, and pain in the elbow was complained of. The stump, which had a livid colour, was extremely sensitive, and at the slightest touch of it the patient almost fainted. Besides this, she showed that peculiar symptom which is by no means rare in persons who have undergone an amputation: that is, she felt pain in the removed part, which increased towards evening. Otherwise she was in fair health, with the exception, however, that she had three years before, after a difficult labour, lost the catamenia, and, in consequence of this, she suffered from headache for a few days every month. I directed a current of the first order of four centimètres power to the left arm, the positive pole being alternately applied to the trunks of the median and ulnar nerves. Direct Faradisation of the muscles, and more especially of the interossei and lumbricals, was also performed. Immediately after the first operation, the patient was again able to bend the second and third phalanges of the fingers; and after three more applications, she was no longer troubled with pain in the removed finger. After the ninth operation, the catamenia re-appeared. The restoration of the mobility of the first phalanges of the fingers required a somewhat longer treatment, as in them the affection was very obstinate; but after some weeks this was also attained. At the same time the stump had assumed a much healthier colour; it was also firmer, and not so sensitive to touch as before. The catamenia continued afterwards at regular intervals.

Case 19. *Reflex Paralysis and Neuralgia of the forearm after fracture.*

M. W., a married woman, aged 46, suffered a fracture of the lower end of the radius of the right arm, in consequence of a fall. She became an out-patient at the Middlesex Hospital, where a bandage was applied; but by the carelessness of the patient, this unfortunately got out of order, and the bone healed crookedly in consequence. It was then again fractured by a surgeon, and put straight; but the cure was now protracted over ten months; and when the bone was at last healed, the arm remained painful and entirely useless. She became, some time afterwards, an out-patient at the Samaritan Free Hospital, and was sent to me by Dr. Henry G. Wright. Faradisation of the median and ulnar nerves was twice performed, when the pain was entirely gone, and the arm could be used as before.

Case 20. Reflex Paralysis after rupture of capsular ligament.

Count Z., aged 63, had, about twenty years ago, suffered from a rupture of the capsular ligament of the hip-joint in consequence of an accident, and had never quite recovered from the effects of it. He complained of great numbness and stiffness in the right leg, the muscles of which were not nearly so well developed as those of the left, so that he had much difficulty in walking. Sir James Clark, whom he had consulted in June, 1857, believed that Faradisation would be the best means to restore him, and sent him to me. The patient was very considerably improved by a short treatment; but, as he left town soon afterwards, the cure was not complete.

Rheumatic Paralysis.

As facial palsy is often caused by a draught of cold air, thus paralysis of the muscles of the extremities is not unfrequently induced by rheumatism. The angler, the huntsman, and others who by pleasure or necessity are much exposed to the changes of temperature, are liable to this kind of palsy, which affects with preference the muscles of the lower extremities, thus giving rise to paraplegia, which is frequently mistaken for a symptom of a disease of the spinal cord. The extensor muscles of the fore-arm, which are animated by the radial nerve, are also often subjected to rheumatic paralysis. Next in frequency ranks paralysis of the deltoid and trapezius, in consequence of which the elevation of the arm becomes difficult or impossible. Finally, the interossei and lumbrical muscles are liable to rheumatic palsy. I have often observed this affection in young ladies, where the first symptom is generally a feeling of numbness in the fingers, and the movements become difficult and troublesome. On faradising the interossei, their excitability generally appears impaired. In such cases it is very easy to arrest the disease by a short faradic treatment; if nothing be done against the affection, the muscles may in time become atrophied; the interosseous spaces appear hollow, the circulation becomes impaired, the hand thin and cold, the fingers can be but slightly removed from each other, and the extension of the two last phalanges is impossible; the numbness and stiffness increases, and at last the hand becomes quite useless.

The invasion of rheumatic paralysis is sometimes sudden, in other cases gradual. It may begin with pain in a set of muscles, whereby motion is rendered difficult or impossible; and when the pain has vanished, the immobility still continues; in other cases no pain, but only numbness, is experienced, which is especially great in the toes, if the seat of the paralysis is in the lower extremities. If the invasion has been sudden, and pain is felt in the paralysed muscles, the electric excitation of the muscles also produces much pain; but when the disease has come on gradually galvanism excites very little sensation.

There is no kind of paralysis in which the therapeutical effects of Faradisation are so striking as in rheumatic paralysis, in which affection it cannot be replaced by any other remedy. This applies also to protracted and severe cases which have resisted a variety of energetical treatment. Thus M. Guitard has related the case of a patient who had suffered for three years from rheumatic paralysis; there was general emaciation and immobility; the head was inclined to the chest, the thighs flexed upon the abdomen, the legs upon the thighs. Faradisation was now practised for a month, and after that time the head could be held erect, and the legs be moved into and out of bed. The faradic treatment was then discontinued for some time, whereupon the patient relapsed into nearly his previous state; it was then recommenced, and at the end of six weeks an almost total recovery had taken place.

I am quite satisfied, that every case of rheumatic paralysis can be cured by Faradisation, provided that the muscular tissue has not yet been destroyed, and the patients do not discontinue the treatment too soon; and even in cases of muscular atrophy resulting from rheumatic paralysis, Faradisation is of great service.

Case 21. *Rheumatic Paralysis of the Fore-arm and Hand.*

Mrs. G., aged 51, was sent to me by Dr. Hyde Salter, in January, 1862. Three months before, she had suffered from a severe attack of rheumatic fever, nearly all the joints having been affected. As soon as she was able to move about again, she went into the country, where her general health much improved. Her right arm and hand, however, remained painful and useless, and she was therefore advised to try Faradisation. On examining the fore-arm and the hand with the æsthesiometer, I found that the sense of touch was considerably diminished. Moreover, there was great waste in all the muscles, more especially in the flexors and the interossei and lumbricals; and on applying an electro-magnetic current to all these muscles individually, it appeared that their sensibility, as well as their contractile power, were very nearly gone. The hand had lost its natural shape, and resembled a bird's claw; a configuration of the hand which is always associated with loss of power in the interossei and lumbrical muscles, and renders it entirely useless. The pain was greatest at night, and chiefly felt in the fingers. The general health of the patient was tolerable, but she was very thin and much depressed. I commenced Faradisation of the skin for the cure of the pain, and of the suffering muscles for restoring them to their normal nutrition and function. After two operations the motor power of the fingers was much increased: the muscles responded more readily to the faradic stimulus, and the æsthesiometer showed an improvement in the sense of touch. The pain, although not entirely gone, was much diminished. After a fortnight's treatment, the patient attending every other day, she was able to feed herself and do some housework, and in a month she could do needlework for three hours consecutively without feeling pain or fatigue. There was then no longer any difference in the sense of touch in the right and left arm, the bulk of the muscles was greatly increased, and the hand had resumed its normal shape. The result was the more satisfactory, as the age and general weakness of the patient were not in favour of a rapid cure.

Traumatic Paralysis.

If the motor nerves are destroyed by mechanical injury, inflammation, or morbid growths invading their substance, the voluntary movements, the sensibility, and the excitability of the muscles to the electric stimulus are more or less impaired, the degree of functional disturbances being directly proportional to the extent of the lesion. If all the fibres of a nerve are destroyed, the properties of the muscles are totally lost. Cases of this kind are incurable, unless a regeneration of nervous matter takes place. It is, however, beyond doubt that in certain cases nerves, which have been divided and have undergone a more or less considerable loss of substance, may be regenerated; and it is proved by microscopic observations of Messrs. Follin, Brown-Séquard, and others, that in cases of this kind there is no interruption of the continuity of the nervous fibrils throughout the cicatrix. If such regeneration of nervous matter has taken place, and the nerves and muscles still remain paralysed, the electric current is the most efficacious means for restoring their lost vitality.

In other cases, where the continuity of the nervous fibres has only been more or less damaged, but not entirely destroyed, there may be loss of power in the muscles, and diminution of their sensibility aud excitability to the electric stimulus. Cases of this kind are more amenable to electricity than such in which the properties of nerves and muscles have been entirely destroyed. Duchenne asserts, that a certain amount of hyperæsthesia, which manifests itself in cases of this kind after the first few applications of electricity, is a favourable sign, as it indicates the commencing return of muscular nutrition; and I have often had the opportunity of verifying this observation. In all such cases electricity should be locally applied to the muscles, the current should be pretty strong and very rapidly interrupted.

Hysterical Paralysis.

In this kind of paralysis neither the nervous centres nor the motor nerves are diseased, although the symptoms may closely resemble those caused by diseases of the brain and of the spinal cord. It occurs in hysterical women, and is brought on either suddenly by anxiety, fright, or excitement, or it creeps on gradually and unawares. Generally the muscles of the lower extremities, and especially the recti of the thighs, are paralysed (hysterical paraplegia), or the muscles of the arm and leg on the same side may be affected (hysterical hemiplegia), or only a single muscle or set of muscles of one limb may suffer. Hysterical paralysis is seldom the only symptom of hysteria in a patient, but it is generally accompanied by globus, hysterical pains, spasms, and disturbances of the menstrual function. Often nothing is apparently more whimsical than the course and the termination of hysterical paralysis. Certain cases get well in a very short time without any medical treatment, others resist for years a variety of energetic therapeutical experiments. In a great number of cases the faradic treatment has yielded splendid results; although it is by no means infallible. As to the mode of application, I may mention, the current should be locally applied to the paralysed muscles, and if this should fail to effect a cure, Faradisation of the skin may be resorted to.

Case 22. *Hysterical Paralysis, Neuralgia, and Loss of Voice.*

M. K., aged 40, a needlewoman of feeble constitution, had for a long time suffered from neuralgia in the right arm, and also from want of power in the muscles, so that she was entirely unable to work. She became an out-patient at the Samaritan Free Hospital, under the care of Dr. Henry G. Wright, who sent her to me. After four operations, in which I directed an extra-current to the weakened muscles, and a current of the first order to the skin for relieving the neuralgia, she was greatly improved; but when she came to me the next time, she had entirely lost her voice. I thereupon directed the faradic stimulus to the recurrent nerve, with the effect that the voice returned at once. By further treatment the patient was entirely cured.

Lead-palsy.

Painters and compositors are most liable to this disease; in the former the blood is poisoned by inhalation of small particles of the powder with which paint is made; or the poison is absorbed through the skin. In the latter the disease is produced by handling printers' types. Not unfrequently lead is taken with adulterated wine or beer; thus lead-palsy often occurs in travellers for wine-merchants; the poison may also get into the blood with the water which has passed through leaden tubes, or with snuff which has been packed in lead-foil. If the blood has become contaminated with lead, various disturbances in the system are produced; such as colics, cramps, amaurosis, neuralgia, paralysis. Paralysis attacks with preference the upper extremities; thus M. Tanquerel des Planches saw amongst 113 cases of lead-palsy, 93 cases of palsy of the arms, 14 of the lower extremities, and 6 of general paralysis. Certain sets of muscles are more liable to this kind of palsy than others. The extensors of the right fore-arm are most liable to it; therefore the wrist drops and cannot be extended; the power of extension of the first phalanges of the fingers is also gone; but the motion of the two last phalanges is not impaired, as the interossei scarcely, if ever, suffer from lead-palsy. The muscles generally soon undergo atrophy, the back of the fore-arm appears concave, the thenar eminence flattened, and the triceps and deltoid may also become more or less wasted. The electric contractility of these muscles is either totally gone, or considerably diminished; but the sensibility is generally preserved. Faradisation is the most efficacious remedy for lead-palsy, and should always be resorted to in cases of this kind; it is even useful if the bulk of the muscles is considerably diminished, and if the muscles do not respond to the faradic stimulus.

PARAPLEGIA ARISING FROM DISEASES OF THE URINARY ORGANS.

Incomplete paralysis of the lower extremities may arise from diseases of the urinary organs, such as nephritis, abscesses of the kidney, renal calculus, inflammation, and ulceration of the mucous membrane of the bladder, enlargement of the prostate, stricture of the urethra, etc. In such cases the discharge of the urine is more or less impeded; the sphincter ani is also weak, the digestion deranged, the limbs very feeble, and the muscular sense nearly lost. The degree of the weakness in the legs varies with the state of the urinary organs. Frequently the paraplegia disappears soon after the impediment to the discharge of the urine is removed; but if the paralysis still persists after the removal of its cause, a faradic treatment is of the most essential use.

5. *Wasting Palsy* (*Cruveilhier's Atrophy*).

This formidable disease, on which we have lately received an able essay by Dr. Roberts, is mainly produced by malnutrition of the muscles, which are progressively destroyed, while the nervous system may be quite healthy, or is only secondarily affected. The disease does not equally attack all the muscles united to a set, but falls apparently capriciously on this or that individual bundle of muscle. Such muscles generally appear of a pale yellow; they are more or less wasted, and often reduced to thin cords. Fat, which is always produced in the retrogressive metamorphosis of tissues, may become accumulated, and take the place of the muscular fibres; in such cases there is not much emaciation, and the limbs may even appear more bulky than formerly;

in other instances the fat is eliminated as soon as formed, and then the limbs are shrunk to the last degree. When the sarcolemma has been destroyed, and the sarcous elements become converted into fat and granular matter, the last ramifications of the motor nerves generally become affected in their turn; in some instances this affection spreads to the anterior roots of the spinal nerves, and even atrophy of the cord may finally be the consequence; but this is never the cause, but only the consequence, of the primary affection of muscular tissue.

The disease mostly affects adult males; but females and infants are not spared. It generally arises from overwork, or anything that over-fatigues the muscles; also from exposure to cold, or from contusions; in some instances there is an hereditary taint, and several members of the same family are affected; while in a great number of cases no palpable cause of the complaint can be ascertained. The disease is almost invariably of slow invasion, and is only discovered by the feeling of loss of power, which is experienced after a great deal of injury has already been done. The loss of power is quite proportional to the degree of atrophy in the muscles. When by the loss of power the patient's attention is drawn to the state of the muscles, he discovers that they are wasted. Besides, rapid quiverings of the individual muscular bundles are perceived, which are never painful, and do not occasion motion in the limb. These quiverings do not accompany all cases of wasting palsy; but if observed, they indicate that the disease is advancing; if they cease, the disease is arrested, or the muscle has become totally destroyed. Many patients also complain of real cramps, which are distinct from these quiverings, and which occur especially during the night in the adductors of the thighs, so that the legs are shaken towards each other, and the patient is prevented from sleep.

There are two forms of this disease, the *partial* and the *general* form. The general form begins either in the upper or in the lower extremities, and as it almost always spreads to the trunk, threatens life. The partial form is not necessarily fatal, but it may pass into the general form, and thus ultimately cause death; it begins either in the hand or in the shoulder, generally of the right side, and may destroy many muscles of the upper extremity, while in the general form all the voluntary muscles throughout the body may be affected by it, with the exception only of the muscles of the eyeball and the muscles of mastication.

If the disease begins in the hand, the muscles of the thumb are generally the first affected; the thenar eminence becomes replaced by a flattened hollow space between the first and second metacarpal bones; afterwards the interossei and lumbricals and the hypothenar eminence become affected. From the hand the disease spreads to the fore-arm; the extensors of the fore-arm are especially liable to this affection, so that the fingers are generally slightly bent, but the flexor muscles may also be destroyed, and in this case the two last phalanges cannot be bent, so that the patient is unable to grasp or seize anything with the hand.

In other instances wasting palsy first invades the muscles of the shoulder, and attacks with preference the trapezius, the serratus magnus, the rhomboidei, and other muscles which unite the scapula to the trunk; the scapula is consequently displaced and twisted round its axis; its upper angle is depressed by the weight of the arm, while the lower angle is raised and projects one or two inches from the surface of the thorax. From the shoulder the disease spreads towards the arm, destroying the deltoid and biceps; thereby the acromion and the coracoid process become prominent under the skin, and serious functional disturbances are the necessary consequence. Although the patient generally learns, in the course of time, to manœuvre very cleverly so as to compel muscles which have escaped destruction to do the work of such as have been wasted, he is at last no longer able to raise his arm or to bend the elbow-joint; he can no longer dress and feed himself; he experiences considerable difficulty in putting on his hat or drawing a handkerchief from his pocket.

If the muscles of the lower extremities are attacked, walking becomes difficult; and at last motion becomes quite impossible. The muscles of the chest, chiefly the pectoralis major, become affected in their turn; the chest appears shrunk, especially beneath the collar-bones.

A certain sign that the disease will shortly prove fatal is destruction of the facial muscles; the physiognomy loses all expression; the saliva is sometimes seen to flow involuntarily; the laryngeal muscles are likewise affected, articulation becomes slow and difficult; the muscles of deglutition, and at last the diaphragm, is attacked. This generally closes the scene; the slightest impediment to respiration which may supervene, produces asphyxia.

It is exclusively the voluntary striped muscles which are thus destroyed; all other organs are generally in the best possible condition. There is no gastric derangement, and the intelligence remains undisturbed to the last moment. There is no anæsthesia of the skin; but the patients are often sensitive to cold, and complain of pain or numbness in the limbs.

The disease may thus end in death; but in some instances it is arrested, and even recovery may take place. Recent cases are more likely to recover than such as are of long standing.

In this affection the localised application of induction currents to the muscles is the only means by which we may hope to arrest the progress of atrophy, and to improve the condition of the patient. In causing the muscles to contract individually, more blood is attracted to their tissue, the bulk and heat of the muscles is increased, and this greater afflux of blood affords the possibility of regeneration. But if this result is to be accomplished, the treatment must be persevered in for a long time, even if no palpable amelioration should occur after the first few weeks. That certain cases, especially such as are of the general form, may run their fatal course in spite of a faradic treatment, is no disparagement of the remedy, which cannot be expected to accomplish impossibilities.

C. *Paralytic conditions of organs animated by sympathetic fibres.*

1. *Intestinal atony.*

In cases of *constipation* which are caused by a want of peristaltic motion of the contractile fibre-cells of the intestines, and by loss of power in the abdominal muscles, Faradisation may be very useful, especially if the affection occurs after protracted diarrhœa and the abuse of aperient medicines. In such cases a total abstinence of laxative medicines is generally imperative, and even simple enemata sometimes do mischief; on the contrary, by Faradisation powerful peristaltic movements of the intestines may be induced, without injuring in any way the mucous membrane of the alimentary canal. I have had several cases under my care in which the strongest aperients had failed to induce opening of the bowels, and in which, by the application of induction currents, a ready discharge of the fæces was brought about.

Tympanitic distension of the abdomen is also often the consequence of intestinal atony, and of loss of power in the abdominal muscles; the intestines meet with no resistance to their distension, and often an enormous meteorism is produced. This is frequently observed in hysterical women; also after the partaking of indigestible food; in acute diseases, especially typhus, pneumonia, small-pox, puerperal fever, peritonitis, etc. This tympanitic distension not unfrequently threatens life, as it may produce asphyxia by paralysis of the diaphragm, and compression of the lungs. Different modes of application have been resorted to. M. Becquerel affirms that he has tried the effect of the induced current in many cases of this kind; he placed the positive electrode into the mouth, and the negative into the rectum; and has never seen any benefit derived from it. The method adopted by M. Becquerel is therefore not to be employed, as it is both inconvenient and useless. Dr. Cumming has proposed placing one electrode on the spine, and the other on the abdominal parietes. I generally place both electrodes on different points of the abdominal parietes, and keep up the action of a rather strong current for about ten minutes. As to the position of the poles, it is best to have the current guided towards the anus.

Case 23. *Extreme meteorism after ovariotomy.*

A married woman, aged 37, mother of one healthy child, 22 months old, came from Aberdeen in April, 1863, to consult Mr. Spencer Wells for a large ovarian tumour, which had begun to form in July, 1862, and had very rapidly increased after August of the same year. The patient had a dark and rather sallow complexion, and had become much emaciated during the last two months. The tongue was clean, the appetite pretty good, her bowels were naturally open, but she complained of troublesome flatulence. The breathing was very little affected, there was no cough and no expectoration. The catamenia had ceased in September, 1862. The pulse was at 120. The girth at the umbilical level was 49 inches. She had been tapped seven times, but had always refilled rapidly. Mr. Wells performed ovariotomy upon her on the 29th of April. There were strong and extensive parietal adhesions, both anteriorly and laterally; 33 pints of fluid were removed, and the cyst and solid matter taken away weighed 13 pounds 13 ounces. Without going further into the details of the case, I merely mention that the patient went on fairly, excepting the immense distension of the stomach and bowels by gas, which was so great as to threaten life. After the most efficacious medicines had been taken, and there was still no improvement, Mr. Wells believed that Faradisation was necessary, and requested me to see the patient. I saw her on the 18th of May, when the flatulent distension was so great that the left lung was almost entirely compressed, the heart being dislodged to the right, and there being tympanitic sound in the second intercostal space. I performed Faradisation, after which the patient had a considerable discharge of flatus. On May 19th, I repeated the operation, and the patient then had two motions, one of them solid. I operated upon her four times more, after which the lung had again expanded to its normal volume, and the patient being nearly well, I discontinued the treatment. On May 26th she went on board the steamer which was to sail the day following for Dundee. The patient died at home in the commencement of August from malignant disease, which had very rapidly formed; but both Mr. Spencer Wells and Dr. Jenner, who had also seen the case, were of opinion that if she had not been faradised, she would have died in London from the effects of the meteorism.

Paralysis of the bladder.

In paralysis of the bladder, which arises from diseases of the nervous centres, the application of electricity to that organ can only have temporary beneficial effects; but where the affection comes on slowly without any apparent cause, in old persons, or in women after labour, or where it is produced by over-distension of the bladder from occasional retention of the urine, Faradisation often proves curative. The same holds good for incontinence of urine in children, especially where this arises from mere atony, and not from irritability of the bladder.

Club-foot.

In some forms of *club-foot*, in which the deformity is caused by paralysis of the muscles on the front of the leg, the same stimulus, directed to the weakened muscles, proves beneficial. In pes planus, where the sole has lost its normal vault, Faradisation of the peroneus longus muscle should be performed.

CHAPTER IV.

SPASMS.

In certain spasmodic diseases, such as chorea, spasm of writers, spasmodic wry-neck, and hysterical cramps and contractions, both Faradisation and Galvanisation may be of the most essential use.

Chorea, which is generally brought on by terror, fright, rheumatism, or intestinal derangement, is frequently seen to disappear after a time without any treatment whatever; other cases get well by cold affusions to the spine, or the internal administration of strychnine, iron, iodide of potassium, etc. Faradisation of the suffering muscles is an excellent remedy for almost all cases of chorea. The effects are mostly immediate, and the muscles become steadier as soon as they are brought under the full influence of Faradisation. Children generally bear the operation remarkably well, as it is not necessary to employ a strong current, a gentle application being quite sufficient.

Spasmodic wry-neck occurs mostly in adults, and can therefore scarcely be considered as a form of chorea. It consists of a convulsive affection of the spinal accessory nerve of one side, whereby the sterno-cleido-mastoid and the trapezius muscles are thrown into commotion. Electricity of high tension as a counter-irritant, and induction currents methodically applied to the antagonists of the suffering muscles, have effected amelioration or cure. The continuous current is chiefly useful in cases where the antagonists of the suffering muscles have not been impaired in their nutrition.

Case 24. *Wry-neck and Dysmenorrhœa.*

On the 21st of November, 1859, I was consulted by a lady, aged 34, who had for about eighteen months suffered from spasmodic contractions of the left trapezius and cleido-mastoid muscles. She observed the first symptoms after a violent emotion, caused by witnessing an accident in the street. At first the contractions were slight, and only occurred if the patient was excited, when in society, or suddenly spoken to. The affection gradually increased and became more troublesome. When she carried the fork or spoon to the mouth, the head at once turned away; at the same time a feeling of numbness, stiffness and fatigue was observed in the left side of the neck; but there was no pain, unless the contractions were unusually violent. She was at first treated by blisters to the neck, and purgatives, but she did not experience any benefit from them. At a later period of her illness, she consulted the late Dr. Todd, who prescribed the valerianate of zinc, in two-grain doses, twice a day; and she thought she had observed a slight improvement after it; but as, after having taken it regularly for two months, she was still a severe sufferer from her complaint, by the advice of Dr. Todd she came to me for Faradisation.

On making an examination of the muscles of the neck, I found the left trapezius and cleido-mastoid somewhat rigid. The corresponding muscles on the right side did not show any signs of atrophy, but on applying the faradic current to the two sets, the excitability of the fibres appeared greater on the left than on the right side; and the sensation excited by the application of the current was also more considerable on the left side. While I was examining the muscles, violent spasms occurred in those affected; the head was convulsively thrown towards the left side, and all the patient's endeavours to keep it straight were of no avail; but by Faradisation of the antagonistic muscles, I at once succeeded in restoring the equilibrium between the two sets, and calming the spasms. I afterwards practised Faradisation of the skin, which I had previously found to be of great benefit in hysterical convulsions. The influence of emotion in exciting the spasms was most striking in this case. The patient suffered far less when she was alone, and if the room was darkened; but if she thought herself observed and the object of wonder or pity, she became much worse. She had, therefore, almost retired from society, and was only with difficulty induced to leave her rooms, from which she used to shut out the light. As eating was troublesome, she took as little food as possible, and, in consequence of this, and the melancholic turn of mind caused by her affection, her general health had become impaired, and the catamenia were very scanty. Faradisation was continued for three days, when the catamenia appeared before the time, and unusually abundant, so that the treatment had to be discontinued for a week. After that it was recommenced, and in a month's time the equilibrium between the two sets of muscles was so entirely re-established, that not a trace of the spasms was observed, even when the patient was excited in any way. The general health also improved in consequence of the changed mode of life now adopted by the patient, and the catamenia again became normal.

Case 25.

On the 6th of May, 1861, I was consulted by a brewer from Hampshire, aged 40, a strong healthy man, who, with the exception of what he described as bilious head-ache, from which he now and then suffered, had never been ill before the present affection came on. In February last, he first noticed that his head was inclined to fall towards the left side. He was unable to assign any exact cause, but mentioned that some time before he first fell ill, while driving, his horse fell and broke his neck, which gave him a great shock. He had also had much anxiety lately, and admitted having slept on a damp couch shortly before being attacked by the spasms. The latter affected the left side of the neck, and gradually became so much worse that he was constantly obliged to hold his head in the right position with the left hand, so that the latter became in a

Faradisation; in the remaining two cases amelioration was produced, and a cure would have been probably effected if the patients had not discontinued the treatment too soon. As generally all other means fail to effect a cure in this troublesome affection, a trial of electricity cannot be too strongly recommended in it.

Hysterical Spasms and Contractions.

In these affections neither the nervous centres nor the motor nerves and muscles are palpably injured, and they are consequently more amenable to electricity than other spasms which are due to affections of the brain and spinal cord. Induction currents of considerable tension sent right through the body by means of foot-baths are an excellent remedy. Not only do they remove the spasms, but they also soothe the general irritability of the system, and procure sleep.

CHAPTER V.

ANÆSTHESIA.

The various forms of electricity have a considerable action upon the sentient nerves. Sparks taken from the common electrical machine while in action, produce a sharp pungent sensation in the skin. The discharge of a Leyden jar through the human body causes a peculiar stunning sensation, known as the electric shock. A continuous galvanic current, when applied to the skin, excites a sensation of heat and pain not only at the commencement and at the cessation of the current, but also during the whole time that the circuit remains closed. If the action of the current be kept up for a certain time, the pain disappears, and a feeling of numbness is perceived. Marianini has taken much trouble in investigating the influence which the direction of the current, when applied to sentient nerves, has in the production of the physiological effects; and he arrived at the conclusion that the sensation, caused by the application of the continuous current, is strongest on making the inverse and on breaking the direct current; while the contrary takes place when the motor nerves are acted upon, as muscular contractions are more easily excited on making the direct and on breaking the inverse current. Therefore, if mixed nerves are excited, the phenomena will be as follows:—

Direct.		Inverse.	
Making	Breaking	Making	Breaking
Contraction	Sensation	Sensation	Contraction

If induction currents are caused to act upon the skin, sensations are produced, varying according to the intensity of the current, and passing through all intermediate degrees, from a slight tickling, burning, or pricking, to the acutest pain; but these sensations almost entirely cease after the circuit has been broken. Besides, the physiological effect is different according to the greater or less velocity of the intermittences. A rapidly-interrupted induced current has more effect on the sentient nerves than a slowly-interrupted current; the reason of this is, that sentient nerves have the property of feeling the effect of impressions some time after they have been acted upon. Thus, if a sentient nerve in its normal condition is subjected to the action of a single induced current of low tension, the sensation caused by it will be trifling; but if a second shock rapidly succeeds the first, the sensation will be much more marked; because the sentient nerve is no longer in its normal physiological condition when it receives the second shock from an induction apparatus, but in an excited state; a third shock will have still more effect than the second, and so on. Therefore it is easy to understand why the sensations produced by the interrupted current increase in direct proportion to the velocity of the intermittences; if a hundred shocks are applied to a sentient nerve within a second, the effect will be quite different from that produced by the same number of shocks, if applied within ten minutes. If the velocity of the intermittences is very great, and an interrupted current sent for a certain time through the trunk of a nerve, a maximum of excitation is reached; after which the excitability of the nerve is diminished, and a direct reduction of its sensibility follows.

The question whether hyperæsthesia may be reduced, and anæsthesia caused by electricity, has of late much occupied the professional mind. It was alleged, that teeth might be extracted without pain by the aid of galvanism, and that even in severe surgical operations electricity might be of service as a local anæsthetic. These assertions are without any foundation; but experiments which I have performed upon myself and others, have shown that if a continuous, or a rapidly-interrupted induced current of medium intensity is sent through the trunk of a nerve,—say the ulnar, or the sciatic, by placing one moistened conductor connected with the positive pole to a point of the skin where the trunk of such nerve is superficial; and another moistened conductor connected with the negative pole to any of the terminal branches of the nerve, and the action of the current be kept up for a quarter of an hour, the pain which is excited by this proceeding becomes much less, after a certain time, than it was at the beginning of the operation, and a feeling of numbness is produced in the limb. I do not mean to say that sensibility can be entirely destroyed by this local application of electricity; but I am quite satisfied that it is notably diminished by it. The result is much more striking, if there is a morbid increase of sensibility in a nerve, as is the case in neuralgia, than if a nerve in its normal state is acted upon.

In a very able paper on the therapeutic uses of electricity, in the British and Foreign Medico-Chirurgical Review for January, 1859, it is contended, that for the relief of hyperæsthesia a current of very high tension is necessary; with this my experience disagrees, as I have seen in many cases, that a current of medium intensity is quite capable of producing the desired result, providing the action of the current be kept up for a certain length of time. If the nerve is in an hyperæsthetic state, I have seldom found it necessary to prolong the application of the current beyond five or six minutes; but to effect a direct reduction of the sensibility of a nerve in its normal condition, the current must act for not less than a quarter of an hour; and in some persons even a longer time will be required.

Independently of the direction of the current, the negative pole of a voltaic pile and of induction machines has a stronger effect on the nerves of the skin than the positive pole. This circumstance may even enable us to tell the direction of the current in an electrical apparatus, provided that certain precautions be taken. It is necessary, in the first place, that similar or nearly similar parts of the skin should be acted upon; since the epidermis is not of the same thickness on all parts of the body, and electricity is less strongly felt where the epidermis offers much resistance to the passage of the current; besides, the distribution of sentient nerves is not equal in all parts of the skin, and electricity will, *cæteris paribus*, be felt more on such parts of the skin, as are richly endowed with nervous filaments, as is the face, than on parts which possess less abundant ramifications. It is also essential that the size and condition (moist or dry) of the conductors should be equal, since a current of the same power possesses more density if conveyed by a small electrode, than if transmitted by a conductor with large surface; and a moist conductor will act less on the skin and more on the muscles, while a dry conductor will act more on the skin and less on the muscles. If, however, the precautions just described be taken, it is easy to distinguish the negative pole from the positive pole, by the stronger sensation excited by the former. Frequently it happens that no sensation whatever is produced by the positive pole, and the negative pole is the only one that is felt. I have verified this fact on many of my patients, who have almost invariably been able to tell the direction of the current, after they had been informed that the strongest sensation is excited at the negative pole.

The difference alluded to is especially remarkable if the feet of the patient are plunged in two basins filled with water, and connected with the poles of the apparatus; in this instance the current is always felt more strongly in that limb in which it is upward. If the hands are plunged into the basins, this effect is not quite so evident, as the epidermis of the right hand is generally thicker than that of the left, in consequence of the greater use made of the right hand. Thus, if the current is upward in the left arm, the sensation will be much stronger in the left than in the right hand; but if the current be upward in the right, the sensations will be nearly the same in both hands, as the more powerful stimulus conveyed to the right hand is compensated by the greater resistance of the epidermis to the passage of the current.

Anæsthesia may be caused by structural diseases of the nervous centres, and of the sentient nerves; and in such cases the electric current can be of use only after the original lesion has subsided. Faradisation is more likely to be successful if the affection is idiopathic, rheumatic, of hysterical origin, or produced by poisoning.

Hysterical Anæsthesia.

Hysterical women often complain of a *sensation of numbness*, which is sometimes fixed in a limb, or part of a limb, in other instances wanders about the body. Cases of this kind are generally speedily cured by electricity. Thus I may mention the case of a woman, aged 36, who was sent to me by Dr. Henry G. Wright; she complained of a sensation of numbness, especially in the nape of the neck, and the dorsal region of the spine; and also in both arms. I applied a mild induced current to the parts mentioned, and when I saw the patient the following day, she stated that she had nearly regained the normal feeling in them; three other operations effected a complete cure. In other instances, however, a longer treatment may be required.

Case 26. *Hysterical Anæsthesia and Paraplegia.*

Ann C., aged 28, married, Carlisle ward, St. Mary's Hospital, under the care of Dr. Alderson.

Three years ago she suffered from rheumatism. Fifteen months ago the first symptoms of her present illness appeared; her walking became difficult, and she did not feel the ground, and a continual sensation of numbness in the back and the lower extremities was complained of. She has never suffered from cramps, or twitches in the leg; she has always been regular. She has been treated by cuppings, leeches, and blisters all along the spine; strychnia, calomel, bandages, and galvanism. When I first saw her, July 5, 1857, the state of sensation was as follows: the skin of the face, the neck, and the arms, had preserved its normal sensibility; on the back there was anæsthesia, from the seventh cervical vertebra down to the sacrum; the prick of a pin is not felt at all in the middle line of the spine, nor on the lower extremities: her gait is staggering, and the muscles of the lower extremities respond very little to the electric stimulus. There are no disturbances in the function of the bladder and the rectum.

In order to restore the lost vitality to the sentient nerves, I applied a current of high tension by means of wires lodged in metallic cylinders to the skin of the back, and of the lower extremities.

While in the normal state of the nerves the faradic stimulus is felt as soon as applied, this patient did not feel it until it had been applied from five to six seconds. Such was the case as well on the back as on the lower extremities; but on the soles of the feet no sensation was to be excited, even by a most intense current. I continued Faradisation, and after six operations the sensation on the back had become nearly normal. The sentient nerves of the lower extremities were more deeply impaired than those of the back, and it took a longer time to produce amelioration in them. The muscles became also much strengthened by the treatment. The patient walked much steadier when she left the Hospital, although she had not quite recovered.

Anæsthesia produced by poisoning.

If anæsthesia is caused by *poisoning* with chloroform, opium, or other narcotic substances, the electric stimulus is one of the most efficacious means of rousing patients from insensibility. Experiments on chickens, pigeons, rabbits, guinea-pigs, and other animals, have shown that when anæsthesia had been produced by ether or chloroform, they were readily aroused by Faradisation. Clinical experience has also proved its utility in cases of this kind. In chloroform-poisoning the electric current can be directed by acupuncture needles to the right ventricle, as the right cavities of the heart are always distended with blood if animation is suspended by chloroform; and if the right ventricle is stimulated to contract, animation may be restored. But the safer plan is to direct the current by metallic wires to the sentient nerves of the skin; and to faradise the phrenic nerve by moistened conductors, in order to produce artificial respiration. Care must be taken, however, that the current administered should not be of very high tension, as otherwise the weakened animation might be entirely destroyed.

Anæsthesia of the nerves of special sense.

All the different forms of electricity are capable of exciting the nerves of special sense; the effect, however, is much more remarkable, if we employ the continuous current than if frictional electricity or the induced current is used. If the induced current be employed, differences are to be observed according as we use the current induced by voltaic electricity or the current induced by a permanent magnet of steel; when both are of the same intensity, the magneto-electric current will have more effect on the organs of sense, and more especially upon the retina, than the electro-magnetic current; which is probably due to the circumstance, that the variations of the magneto-electric current are not so sudden and considerable as those of the current induced by voltaic electricity. If we use the interrupted current for exciting the retina, it must possess a high tension, or no effect would be produced; therefore the current induced in a long and fine wire (induced current, properly so called, or Duchenne's current of the second order) would best answer our purpose. In regard to the direction of the current, I may mention that the *positive* pole acts more on the retina and on the tongue than the negative pole; but if an electric current is made to act upon the ear, the effect will be stronger if the *negative* pole be applied to it.

1. *Organ of vision.*

If the continuous current of a single pair is caused to act upon the optic nerve, one of the metals being placed to the conjunctiva or to the eyelid well moistened, and the other metal to the other eye or eyelid, a flash of light is perceived, which is strongest at the commencement of the current; while the circuit is closed, the luminous appearances are much less intense, but they become more distinct again when the circuit is broken. I need scarcely mention this is no real development of light, but that the flash is only seen by the one subjected to the experiment in consequence of the vital energy of the optic nerve being excited by galvanism.

Sparks taken from the common electrical machine and applied to the eyes, produce also luminous appearances, although not very distinct. The extra-current of an induction machine, which is produced in a short and thick wire, and possesses, therefore, a low tension, does not affect the retina in the least; while the current induced in the fine wire acts upon it in direct proportion to its tension.

The flash of light perceived in consequence of the galvanic excitation of the retina appears coloured; it is bluish, when the positive pole is applied nearest to the eye; and Ruete observed that, in this case, the sensation of light is strongest at a point which corresponds to the macula lutea, becoming gradually darker as it approaches the periphery of the field, while if the negative pole is directed to the eye, a yellow-reddish or orange-coloured light is perceived, which appears strongest in the periphery of the field, and gradually darkens towards the centre.

The luminous appearances take place by reflex action from the sentient fibres of the trigeminal nerve to the retina. They may therefore be perceived, whatever may be the position of the poles, provided that one of them touches a point of the skin or mucous membrane animated by a filament of the fifth pair. It is, therefore, unnecessary to touch one or both eyeballs or eyelids; we may perceive the flash, for instance, if one pole be directed to the Schneiderian membrane, and the other to the mucous membrane of the cavity of the mouth. Mr. George Hunter observed that, by placing one of the metals as high up as possible between the gums and the upper lip, and the other in a similar situation with respect to the lower lip, a flash was produced as vivid as that occasioned by passing one of the metals up the nose and placing the other upon the tongue.* It differs, however, from

* Experiments and Observations relative to the Influence lately discovered by M. Galvani, and commonly called Animal Electricity. By Richard Fowler. Edinburgh, 1793, p. 64.

the flash produced in any other way, by the singular circumstance of not being confined to the eye alone, but appearing diffused over the whole of the face. The flash may be also perceived, if one pole is placed in the mouth and the other in the rectum: this experiment was first made by M. Achard, of Berlin.*

The flash becomes more distinct and of a stronger colour on darkening the room, and Humboldt relates that, during storms, the effect of galvanism upon the eyes is most remarkable. I may also mention that Fowler made the experiment on himself at a time when one of his eyes was inflamed, and noticed that the flash produced in the inflamed eye was much more considerable than in the uninflamed eye. On the other hand, Humboldt states that he made the experiment when he was affected by a very bad cold; and that then he was not able to perceive the flash at all, even if he made use of an otherwise most efficacious arrangement.

The intensity of the flash is directly proportional to the intensity of the current employed,

* Versuche über die gereizte Muskel und Nervenfaser. Von Alexander von Humboldt. Posen und Berlin, 1797, vol. i. p. 334.

and inversely proportional to the resistance offered to the passage of the current. A flash is produced by a very feeble current, such as is excited by a half-crown piece and a penny; it is more distinct if, instead of copper and silver, tinfoil and silver, or zinc and gold, are used. The excitation of the retina produced by a pile consisting of a number of pairs, is very violent, and instantaneous blindness may ensue from it. Duchenne, who was unacquainted with the power of the continuous current to excite the retina in this remarkable manner, relates a case, which fully proves the practical importance of the knowledge of the physiological effects which electricity will invariably produce. He galvanised a patient suffering from paralysis of the portio dura, at first by the interrupted current, and afterwards by the continuous current of a pile. Immediately after the electrodes of the pile had been applied to the face, the patient exclaimed that he saw the whole room in a blaze; he afterwards complained of having lost his sight on that side where the electrodes had been applied; and he never regained it. Duchenne claims for himself the discovery of the special action of galvanism on the retina; but this was already known to Volta, before the commencement of the present century.

If the resistance to the passage of the current be great, the flash perceived in consequence of the galvanic excitation of the retina will be very feeble. Thus, if the two metals are applied to the face at two points where the skin is quite dry, the flash will be far less vivid than if the skin be previously moistened. Besides, the flash will be stronger if the electrodes are directed to the conjunctiva, or to the Schneiderian membrane, or to the mucous membrane of the cavity of the mouth, than if they are applied to the skin of the face; since the delicate epithelium of the mucous membranes offers much less resistance to the passage of the current than the epidermis.

Amaurosis.

Amaurosis has been often treated by galvanism, and M. Magendie has been fortunate enough to cure cases of this kind. It is obvious that we cannot hope to succeed, if the amaurosis is caused by disease of the brain, or of the organ of vision, or if it is the result of Bright's disease and diabetes: but only if it is due to anæsthesia of the optic nerve. As the continuous current has a special action on the retina, this form of electricity should be used (a current of about six pairs of Bunsen's battery); the employment of induction currents is also allowable, and in this case the magneto-electric current best answers the purpose. Moistened electrodes may be applied to any part of the face, as the action on the retina takes place by reflex from the trigeminal to the optic nerve. It is quite unnecessary to employ electro-puncture, which generally frightens the patients, and is connected with many inconveniences. The operations should be short and often repeated. An examination of the eye by means of the ophthalmoscope should always precede the commencement of the galvanic treatment, as many cases which are said to be amaurosis really depend upon morbid changes in the retina, chorioidea, etc., which absolutely prevent the possibility of vision.

2. *Organ of smell.*

It is a well-known fact that frictional electricity gives rise to a peculiar smell, which is not exactly that of phosphorus, but half sulphurous and half phosphoric. It was formerly believed that this odour was due to a peculiar state of the olfactory nerve excited by electricity; but we now know, from the researches of Professor Schönbein and others, that the odour arises from the presence in the air of ozone, which is formed out of hydrogen and oxygen under the influence of electricity. The odour of ozone is hardly ever perceived near voltaic piles and induction machines; this is due to the circumstance that voltaic, as well as induction sparks, are always accompanied with a development of heat, by which ozone is destroyed as soon as liberated.

Neither the common electric sparks, nor the continuous, nor the interrupted current (if they are not of great intensity), have any remarkable effect in exciting a peculiar smell when applied to the mucous membrane of the nose. By applying electricity to the Schneiderian membrane, in all cases a more or less painful scratching and tickling is caused, owing to the irritation of the sentient nerves, with which this membrane is richly endowed; sometimes sneezing, as reflex movement follows the application of electricity to the nose.

Ritter is the only observer who has experimented with a very intense electric current upon his own Schneiderian membrane. He used a current generated by a voltaic pile of twenty pairs; the inconvenience caused to him by the experiment was very great. He gives, as the result of his researches, that a peculiar smell is excited, not only at the commencement of the current, but also while the circuit remains closed; besides at the cessation of the current, and a certain time after the circuit has been broken. The effects are different according to the direction of the current. If it be inverse, we observe at the commencement of the current, and while the circuit is closed, an acid smell and loss of the capability of sneezing; at the cessation of the inverse current, and a short time after the circuit has been broken, we perceive an ammoniacal smell and disposition to sneezing. If, on the other hand, we employ the direct instead of the inverse current, the contrary is perceived, viz., ammoniacal smell and disposition to sneezing on establishing the circuit, and while the current continues to pass; and an acid smell and loss of the capability of sneezing, on breaking the circuit, and a short time after it has been broken.

Loss of Smell.

Loss of smell is often to be traced to morbid changes affecting the olfactory nerve, which may be compressed by exostosis, tumours, etc. I have seen a case in which the loss of smell evidently arose from over-excitation of the olfactory nerve, as the patient had for many years been in the habit of taking more than an ounce of very strong snuff every day, and the smell had very gradually disappeared. This might have been a good case for an electric treatment, which I proposed to the patient; but he would not submit to it.

3. *Organ of hearing.*

If the drum of the ear is galvanised, sounds are heard by the one subjected to the experiment. The best way to effect this is to fill the external opening of the ear with warm water; a metallic conductor, connected with the negative pole of a battery, or an induction apparatus, is then held in the liquid, and the circuit is closed by placing another moistened conductor on the nape of the neck.

The drum of the ear is equally excitable by the continuous and the induced current. If we make use of the continuous current, sounds are produced not only at the commencement of the current, but also while the circuit remains closed. Volta relates, in a letter to the Right Honourable Sir Joseph Banks,* that when he introduced the

* Philosophical Transactions, 1800, p. 423.

poles of a pile of 30 to 40 pairs into the external opening of the ear, he felt a shock to his head, and some moments afterwards he heard a sound, or rather a noise, like scratching and bubbling, or like that of a viscid substance boiling. This noise continued without interruption, and became even more intense until the circuit was broken. But we may produce sounds by means of a much feebler current, such as is produced by a battery of three to four pairs. The effect is always strongest if the negative pole is applied to the ear.

The action of the induced current upon the drum of the ear presents some differences according to the intensity of the current, and to the greater or less velocity with which the intermittences succeed each other. A single shock from an induction apparatus produces a noise like a scratch; if the shocks succeed each other rapidly, the noises do so likewise, and then resemble the buzzing of a fly on a window, or the blowing of a distant trumpet. At the tame sime a sensation of tickling, and even pain, is perceived, if the current be of high tension.

Ritter has taken much trouble to distinguish the pitch of the tone produced by the galvanic excitation of the drum of the ear. He states that, when both his ears were enclosed in the circuit, at the commencement of the direct current he felt a strong shock, and heard the sound G. This persisted as long as the direct current continued to circulate; if the intensity of the current was augmented, the sound became higher than G. On the contrary, when the inverse current was used, the sound was lower than G, and continued to become lower in proportion as the intensity of the current was increased. Both sound and shock were weak on breaking the circuit, alike when the current was direct or inverse.

I have made a number of experiments with all sorts and directions of currents, and compared the sound produced by the galvanic excitation of the drum of the ear with that given by a tuning fork of the present philharmonic pitch; and I have always found the sound produced by electricity as near as possible to A. I have never observed that by changing the direction of the current, or by increasing its intensity, the *pitch* of the sound was changed; the only difference I have perceived was in the *intensity* of the tone. It was stronger if the negative pole was directed to the ear, and the positive to the nape of the neck, than if the position of the poles was reversed. The tone was hardly perceptible if a current of low tension was used, and very loud if it was of high tension; but the pitch invariably remained the same.

By Galvanisation of the membrana tympani in living man, two other remarkable phenomena are produced, viz., a slight and unpleasant metallic taste, and a more or less abundant flow of saliva.

The production of this peculiar sensation of taste is due to excitation of the trunk of the chorda tympani, which, after having emerged from the cavity of the tympanum through the fissura Glaseri, descends towards the lingual nerve, into the sheath of which it enters, and then further proceeds towards the tongue. It is proved by electro-physiology, that the chorda tympani essentially contributes to the perception of taste; and clinical experience confirms this physiological induction; as in certain cases of paralysis of the portio dura, there is a loss of taste, together with palsy of the muscles of the face; this loss of taste exists only on the affected side, and usually disappears at the same time with the other symptoms of the paralysis of the portio dura. Several cases of this kind have been recorded by Dr. Gull and others.

A not less remarkable phenomenon is the flow of saliva produced by Galvanisation of the drum of the ear. My attention was directed to this fact in the following way: having often been requested to try the effects of galvanism on patients suffering from what is commonly called nervous deafness, I noticed that the patients, during the operation, made movements of deglutition; I then experimented on myself with the view of ascertaining the cause of these movements, and found that, if a current of rather high tension was caused to act upon the chorda tympani, the saliva began to flow more or less abundantly. It is evident that this is due to an electric excitation of those fibres of the chorda tympani, which do not proceed towards the tongue with the lingual nerve, but are detached from the principal part of the chorda tympani, and penetrate into the submaxillary ganglion. The saliva, therefore, which is observed to flow when the chorda tympani is being galvanised, is secreted in the submaxillary gland.

The most recent researches on the physiological action of the continuous galvanic current on the organ of hearing, have been undertaken by Dr. Brenner, of St. Petersburg, who has considerably enlarged our knowledge of these phenomena. He found* that if the negative pole was applied to the ear, the nerve responded to the galvanic stimulus on closing the circuit, and while the current continued to pass, but if the positive pole was in the ear, there was an effect only on opening the circuit. On the other hand, no effect was produced on opening the circuit, if the negative pole was in the ear; nor on closing the circuit or during the time the current passed, if the positive pole was in the ear. The greater the power of the current, the stronger were the sounds heard, viz., varying from the buzzing of a fly, to that of rolling of carriages in the distance, rolling of carriages near the observer, striking of a gong, striking of a bell, etc. The auditory nerve, therefore, answers in the same way to the application of the galvanic current as do the motor nerves. Both poles have a different effect, as regards quality as well as quantity, and this without any regard to the direction of the current. The excitability of the nerve may be increased during the operation, so that the nerve will respond to a lower force of current than it did previously. If the force of the current is increased, the re-action

* Военно-медицинскій журналъ, 1863.

is sooner manifested at the negative than at the positive pole. Dr. Brenner has proposed the following formula as expressing the normal re-action of the auditory nerve.

I. N C S = negative pole; closing; clear, sonorous sound.
N E Rr = negative pole; established circuit; strong resounding, which very gradually disappears.
N O Z = negative pole; opening; zero.

II. P C Z = positive pole: closing; zero.
P E Z = positive pole; established circuit; zero.
P O S = positive pole; opening; clear, sonorous sound, but not as strong as in N C S.

This normal re-action of the auditory nerve appears materially altered in certain morbid conditions of the organ of hearing.

Nervous deafness.

Nervous deafness has often been treated by electricity, and there can be no doubt that certain cases are amenable to it. It is especially that sort of deafness which occurs in hysterical women, and is connected with noises in the ear, which is liable to be beneficially affected by galvanism. I have had twenty-three cases of deafness under my care, and have been assured by fourteen patients that they heard very much better after having been faradised for a certain time. In one case I have been fortunate enough to stop the noises in the ear entirely, while in nine such cases no benefit was afforded. Dr. Brenner's method promises to be successful in all cases where the normal re-action of the auditory nerve to the continuous galvanic current is altered.

Case 27. Deafness treated by Faradisation.

A. M., a married woman, aged 37, mother of three children, of a very delicate constitution and a disposition to consumption, came under my care in October, 1861. The beginning of her deafness dates as far back as 1849, and the only cause she could assign for it was cold. There had never been any inflammation of, nor discharge from, the ear. She had been treated for a long time at St. Thomas's Hospital, but without any benefit. Dr. Wright, who had previously seen good results of Faradisation at my hands in cases of deafness, sent the patient to me. I could not discover any signs of disease in the temporal bone, in the

Eustachian tube, or in the membrana tympani; and it is just such cases of deafness, which are of very frequent occurrence, in which Faradisation generally produces excellent results. The patient was placed in a recumbent position, the external opening of the ear was filled with warm water, and a moistened conductor connected with the positive pole was applied to the nape of the neck, while the negative pole was made to touch the water in the meatus. If the operation is performed in this manner, the whole extent of the membrana tympani is brought under the influence of Faradisation. I applied an extra-current of one centimètre power. Considering the long duration of the affection, the result of the treatment was very remarkable. The patient who, when she came to me, did not notice any questions I addressed to her, nor hear any sounds produced, heard, on leaving my house, after the first operation, a dog dark; and on turning into Oxford-street, she heard the whistle of an omnibus conductor. From that time she steadily improved, so that it soon became easy to converse with her. At the same time the catamenia, which were very scanty, became more abundant and of a better character.

4. *Organ of Taste.*

That a peculiar sensation of taste is perceived when the tongue is touched by two heterogeneous metals, has been known long before the discovery of galvanism. M. Sulzer seems to have been the first whose attention was directed to this fact. In a paper which was published by him in the Reports of the Berlin Academy of Sciences, in 1754,* the following remarks occur: "If a piece of lead and a rod of silver are connected with each other, and approached to different parts of the tongue, a sensation of taste is experienced, which resembles that produced by vitriol of iron; while, if we employ either of the metals alone, not the slightest taste is perceived. It is probable, that by the connection of the two metals a vibration is produced in the smallest particles, either of the lead or of the silver, or of both of them; and that this vibration, which must necessarily affect the nerves of the tongue, produces the taste described." This is in so far interesting, as it is in all proba-

* Recherches sur l'origine des sentimens agréables et désagréables. Histoire de l'Académie des Sciences et Belles Lettres de Berlin. 1754, p. 356.

bility the very first observation ever made on the physiological effects of galvanic electricity.

If we apply a single pair of zinc and silver to the tongue, the zinc being directed to the top, and the silver to the back, of the tongue, a very remarkable acid taste is produced under the zinc plate, and a feeble alkaline taste under the silver plate. These sensations are not only perceived at the commencement and at the cessation of the current, but also as long as the circuit is closed, The effect is most distinct when the tongue is at its ordinary temperature, and when the metals are of the same temperature as the tongue. When either the metals, or the tongue, or both, are heated or cooled, as far as can be borne without inconvenience, scarcely any sensation is produced; and whatever has a tendency to blunt the sensibility of the tongue, such as acids, pepper, laudanum, spirits, etc., diminishes the effect of galvanism.

If, instead of a single pair, a pile be used, we observe, not only the specific sensation of taste, but also a flash of light, pain in, and convulsions of, the tongue. The interrupted current produces only the latter phenomena, but no peculiar sensation of taste. Frictional electricity, however, has an action on the tongue, which resembles that produced on it by galvanic electricity. Fowler has compared the taste produced by common electric sparks to the taste of vinegar, and that produced by galvanism to the taste of diluted sulphuric acid.

This remarkable affection of the tongue by electricity may be explained in various ways. Thus it may be urged, that the sensation of taste is due to a peculiar state of the gustatory nerve produced by electricity, just as a sensation of light is produced by directing the galvanic stimulus to the retina. But the differences in the taste beneath the different poles seem to lead to the conclusion, that the effect is due to an electrolysis of the salts of the saliva, as from chloride of sodium, which is dissolved in the saliva, muriatic acid would be evolved at the zinc pole,—whence the acid taste; and soda at the silver pole,—whence the alkaline taste. It has been objected to this explanation, that a current, which is too feeble to bring about a decomposition of the salts of the saliva, will produce a remarkable sensation of taste; besides, we know that frictional electricity produces a marked sensation of taste, although its chemical powers are so feeble that it seems scarcely possible to assume an electrolysis of the salts of the saliva by a few electric sparks. Finally, Volta has observed, that an acid taste was perceived under the zinc pole, even when the mucous membrane of the tongue was in contact with an alkaline solution, by which the acid, which might have been formed, would immediately become neutralised, so as to produce no physiological effect whatever.

Professor Schönbein has ventured another explanation.* He supposes that by the galvanic current, air becomes decomposed, and that, at the positive pole, the oxygen and nitrogen combine to form nitric acid; which would produce the acid taste. But Schönbein does not explain the cause of the alkaline taste which is perceived under the silver pole, and it seems doubtful whether the action of one galvanic pair, or of a few and small electric sparks, is sufficiently powerful to produce a decomposition of air. We are, therefore, at present obliged to content ourselves with the following view: that the sensation of taste is probably due to a peculiar state of the gustatory nerves caused by electricity.

* Ueber einige mittelbare physiologische Wirkungen der atmosphärischen Elektricität. Henle und Pfeufer's Zeitschrift. 1851. Heft III. p.385.

Loss of Taste.

In *loss of taste*, the continuous current is probably more efficacious than induction currents, which act only on the sentient nerves of the tongue, but not on the gustatory nerves.

CHAPTER VI.

NEURALGIA.

If hyperæsthesia is caused by wounds of the nerves, by inflammation, hypertrophy, or cancer of the neurilemma, electricity cannot be expected to cure this affection; the same is the case if neuralgia originates in inflammation, caries, exostosis of the bony canals through which the nerves pass, or in diseases of the nervous centres, or in morbid states of the liver, uterus, ovaries, kidneys, etc. But if the neuralgia appears to be merely a morbid exaltation of sènsibility without structural changes, or if it is caused by rheumatism, a galvanic or faradic treatment may be resorted to with a fair chance of success.

From the time when Sarlandière and Magendie first made known their observations on the therapeutical use of galvano-puncture, galvanism has been frequently and in various ways administered for the relief of such neuralgic pains as defy other therapeutical proceedings. The practice of galvano-puncture being connected with more or less inconvenience, viz., in many instances violent pain during the operation, and afterwards inflammation and suppuration in those tissues into which the needles have been thrust, other modes of applying galvanism have therefore been naturally resorted to. Duchenne has recommended Faradisation of the skin, by means of metallic brushes conveying a very powerful electro-magnetic current to the affected points, in order to produce a strong revulsion; but the pain produced by this proceeding is, according to Duchenne himself, very bad, and in a certain number of cases the operation has not been successful. Another, and in my opinion the best, way is to send a continuous or an induced current of medium intensity for a certain time through the affected nerve by means of moistened conductors; as I have shown that, by such a proceeding, a direct reduction of the sensibility in a nerve may be produced. The pain produced by it is insignificant and scarcely worth mentioning, when compared to the often excruciating neuralgic pain against which the proceeding is resorted to. On the other hand, I have seen the method alluded to answering in cases where both electro-puncture and Faradisation of the skin had been practised with little or no success. From a number of patients I have treated for neuralgia, the following cases are subjoined to illustrate the therapeutical proceeding.

Case 28. Tic Douloureux.

Mrs. ——, aged 28, had been in good health until May, 1857, when, in consequence of having got wet through, she was seized by violent pains in the right side of the face, accompanied at first with fever and general indisposition. The latter symptoms soon subsided, but not the very violent shooting pain, which came on in paroxysms, at the end of which the patient was completely exhausted. For the first few weeks the paroxysms came on very irregularly, about four or five in the course of the day; but after some time, an intermittent character was remarked, as only one paroxysm came on every other day between four and five o'clock in the afternoon. Large doses of quinine and arsenic had been given, but without producing the anticipated effect; the patient had also been treated by calomel, sublimate, iodide of potassium, and blisters. Her general health has much suffered; she has become nervous and irritable. When I first saw her, her condition was as follows:—There are always premonitory symptoms which announce the approaching paroxysm, viz., a sort of tickling in the epigastrium, followed by formication in the face. Then very violent pains begin, which are chiefly felt on the zygomatic bone, beneath the lower eyelid, in the cheek and chin, a little less on the nape of the neck, but not in the forehead and the temple. This paroxysm usually lasts about half an hour, and then slowly subsides into a dull pain, which continues for three or four hours. The following day she is free from pain, the third day is again marked by a paroxysm. On examination of the face, I found two of Valleix's painful points, viz., one on the zygomatic bone, where the temporo-malar, and another on the infraorbitar foramen, where the infraorbitar nerve emerges from the orbit: pressure on these two points excited a distinctly painful sensation in the free interval. I therefore thought it well to place the poles alternately on these two points, by means of moistened conductors, conveying a rapidly-interrupted induced current to the suffering nerves. The first application (Oct. 10, 1857,) made at the time when the paroxysm had just commenced, alleviated, according to the patient, the severity of the pain, but did not shorten the duration of the paroxysm. On the 12th of October, another paroxysm came on in due time, and was then positively shortened by Faradisation. On the 14th premonitory symptoms, as usual, but no paroxysm. On the 16th a paroxysm came on which was subdued in five minutes. Five other operations were performed, the last paroxysm having been on the 26th of October. I saw the patient in the beginning of June, 1858, when she told me that up to that time she had not been troubled again by the pain.

The continuous current is, on the whole, equally valuable in the treatment of hyperæsthesia as the induced current; as is illustrated by the following case:—

Case 29. *Tic Douloureux.*

Mrs. L., aged 41, came under my care in August, 1862. She had, for the last twenty-five years, with few intermissions, suffered from tic douloureux, which attacked the left side of the face, especially the temple, cheek, and chin. The pain was most violent from 6 o'clock in the evening till 2 or 3 in the morning, and prevented sleep. It was worse in damp weather, and when easterly winds prevailed. The patient herself had become extremely irritable and hysterical, and was quite out of health. Almost every narcotic had been used for relieving her, but generally with the effect that the pain was increased instead of diminished. This was chiefly the case with opiates, belladonna, and henbane: arsenic and quinine had also been given, but signally failed. I administered a continuous galvanic current of very low tension (four cells of Bunsen's battery) to the two inferior branches of the trigeminal nerve, and ordered at the same time the internal use of Spa water for improving her general health. Three operations, which were most agreeable to the patient, were sufficient to cure her of a disease which had for twenty-five years embittered her life; and up to the present time (December, 1863) no relapse has taken place.

Cases of pain in the back and of inframammary pain in hysterical women are generally cured by a short faradic treatment. The inframammary pain which is in some instances dependent upon incipient lateral curvature of the spine, but more frequently exists without any apparent structural lesion, is generally felt below the left mamma and at the margin of the ribs; I have seen a number of cases of this affection, some associated with amenorrhœa, others not. In those patients who suffered from amenorrhœa, the return of the catamenia and the disappearance of the pain were simultaneous. For inframammary pain a strouger current is generally required than for other neuralgic affections, and the action of the current should be kept up for ten minutes. Clavus hystericus is also amenable to electricity.

In sciatica, Faradisation as well as Galvanisation often prove successful, although the affection is generally more difficult to cure, by any form of electricity, than tic douloureux.

Case 30. *Sciatica.*

J. F. T., aged 35, from Edinburgh, has never been in strong health, and suffered for a long time from acidity in the stomach. Eight years ago he had his left thigh amputated for tumor albus; he carries now an artificial leg, which, being very heavy, exerts a great strain upon the left side of the pelvis. Three years ago, he first began to feel pain on the back of the right thigh, and on the inside of the leg, down to the ankle. The pain having been dull and heavy for some time, soon became keen and acute, so that the patient was laid up by it. He thought it was brought on by his having taken too much exercise. He did not suffer from violent paroxysms of pain, followed by free intervals, but was permanently troubled. He placed himself under the care of two of the most eminent practitioners of Edinburgh, and after some time was much relieved, the acuteness of the pain slowly but gradually subsiding. He then left Edinburgh; but being still troubled, he bad acupuncture practised upon him, needles being thrust into the sciatic nerve. From this proceeding he received immediate relief, but the pain never entirely left him, and was much about the same shortly after the operation. About two years afterwards he came up to town and consulted Sir James Clark, who kindly sent him to me. The pain was dull at that time. When the patient walks, even for a short distance, the pain is much increased, and is also very bad in the first part of the night. Strong pressure has no marked influence upon the pain; but it rather relieves than aggravates it. Besides, the patient states, that early in the morning there are usually lively spasms perceptible in the muscles of the leg, which, however, generally subside in the course of the day; as they are not accompanied with any unpleasant sensations, he rather regards them as a curiosity than as an object to be complained of. I first resolved trying Duchenne's proceeding of Faradisation of the skin, and made use of a powerful current, which I applied by a wire brush to the suffering parts. Two such applications, however, produced no effect. On the third day, I therefore sent a very rapidly interrupted induced current of medium intensity through the sciatic nerve, placing the positive electrode near the tuberosity of the ischium, the negative one near the ankle. Moistened conductors were kept in close contact with the skin, on the points mentioned, for six minutes; and when I interrupted the application, the pain was quite gone, and the patient left me free from any unpleasant sensation. When he called again on the following day, he told me that the pain had returned about three hours after the operation; but that it was by no means so severe as it had been before, and that he had enjoyed a very quiet sleep that night. I repeated this operation three times again, after which he was obliged to leave town. After the second operation, the patient had been free from pain up to the following morning; and, after the fourth, he only felt it very trifling when walking, but not while in a quiescent position. Six weeks afterwards, I received a note from the patient, stating, that since this treatment his limb had been a good deal better. He was, however, not totally free from pain when he walked to any distance; yet the pain went off sooner, was less severe, and not so liable to return as formerly. I, therefore, advised him to come up to town once more, to undergo another course of the same treatment. This the patient did some time afterwards. I operated upon him six times more as above, and with such a beneficial effect that, the patient was no longer troubled, even when walking the considerable distance of three or four miles. I will not forget to mention, that the spasms which used to come on early in the morning, in the muscles of the leg, were not done away with by the electric treatment; but as the patient never found them in any way unpleasant, he did not care for them.

I conclude with a case of neuralgia which was chiefly remarkable for its cause, and its rapid cure. The patient was a merchant, aged 30, of vigorous constitution, and active habits. He was a passenger by the Canadian steamer, which foundered at sea on the 4th of June, 1861, about 200 miles off the coast of Canada. Many of the passengers were drowned; but this gentleman, by means of a life-buoy, was enabled to float until, three-quarters of an hour afterwards, he was picked up by a boat which was passing. Life was then almost extinct. The water was at the time very little above freezing-point, as large masses of ice were floating in it. The patient, however, soon rallied; but unfortunately he had to remain in his wet clothes for a considerable time; and, even when he landed, he could not at once obtain a change of dress. He did not at first experience any ill effects from this accident; but, after some time, he began to feel severe burning pain in the arms and legs; and when the pain subsided, he perceived numbness in the limbs and loss of muscular power. He soon afterwards returned to England, and was, during his passage, subjected to treatment by the ship-surgeon, who prescribed anodyne applications, as opium, aconite, etc., to the arms, and general tonics; but he derived no benefit whatever from the remedies used. On his arrival in this country, he consulted Mr. Snape, of Bolton-le-

Moors, in Lancashire, who gave his opinion, that Faradisation would be the best means of restoring him, and accordingly sent him to me. On examination, I found the following morbid symptoms:—1st, as regards the sentient nerves: there was a burning neuralgic pain, especially in the fore-arms and thighs, which very much increased towards evening and in the night; so that the patient was prevented from sleep, and in consequence became much exhausted in the morning. There was also considerable anæsthesia, especially in the right hand and fore-arm, where the prick of a pin could not be felt at all; while, on other parts, it was only obtusely felt, and not as a prick, but as a mere touch. The sense of touch, especially in the right hand, was also much diminished. Finally, there was a semi-paralytic condition of the arms; the patient could move them, but he had no power over the muscles; he could not grasp anything with force, and experienced great difficulty in writing. The contractility of the muscles was not diminished, as they answered readily to an electric current of moderate power, only the influence of volition over them had considerably decreased. The flexor muscles of the fore-arm were most affected. The general health of the patient was good, notwithstanding the loss of rest, and the wear and tear consequent upon great suffering.

After having examined the patient, I quite agreed with Mr. Snape as to the advisability of resorting to Faradisation, and applied a rapidly-interrupted current of the first order of three centimètres power of my apparatus, to the skin for relieving the neuralgic pain and the anæsthesia; and an extra-current of four centimètres to the weakened muscles, in order to restore their power. The following were the effects of this treatment:— The pain, which was very severe at the time the patient came to me, disappeared during the first application; and he slept soundly the following night. The pain returned in the morning, although in a less degree; and, after a few more applications, in which I modified the intensity of the current and the duration of the operation, according to the necessities of the case, it was entirely subdued. The anaesthesia also yielded rapidly to the means employed. After three operations, the patient was again able to feel distinctly, not only the prick of a pin, wherever I applied it, but also the mere touch of blunt instruments; and when he left town, after having been under my care for six days, he was quite free from pain, the anaesthesia was gone, the sense of touch was again normal, and the muscular power had returned. I have not seen him since; but Mr. Snape has kindly written to say, that the effects of the treatment have been permanent; and that the patient returned to Canada some time ago in perfect health.

THE END.

CPSIA information can be obtained
at www.ICGtesting.com
Printed in the USA
LVHW101347160422
716387LV00003B/225

9 783752 594492